SNATCHED WITH MY STEPBROTHER

SUBMITTING TO MY STEPBROTHER

M. FRANCIS HASTINGS

For my editor who makes sure you get your fix on time.

CONTENTS

1

STRANDED AGAIN

-Jacey-

We stopped before nightfall, as even the conservation officer wasn't stupid enough to go zipping around the lake without the aid of daylight. Ironically, we ended up at our old campground. It was empty now, but at least there was the fire pit where Girard started a fire.

"I'd suggest getting some shut-eye, but I'm pretty sure you won't," Girard said, and the conservation officer snickered.

I leaned against Caleb, both of us out of our life jackets now. Caleb was wearing a T-shirt and a button-down flannel shirt. I wore a Care Bear sweatshirt. Caleb had opened his shirt to tuck me against him and wrap it partially around me. Neither of us answered Girard's stupid statement.

"I've always been curious, Caleb. What's it like to fuck your sister?" Girard chuckled.

The conservation officer perked up. "Oh? What's this now?"

"Jacey and Caleb are brother and sister," Girard informed him.

The conservation officer slapped his knee and let out a great guffaw. "No kidding!"

"Step. Step-siblings," Caleb responded through his teeth. "Her father married my mother when we were teenagers. We're not related."

"And you're gonna be making that distinction all your life," the conservation officer said.

"What's left of it," Girard added. "Yeah, I hear tell they fucked like rabbits when they thought they were going to die. Too bad I wasn't keeping watch that night."

I dug my nails into Caleb's thigh when I felt a growl rumble in his chest. I didn't want him to do anything stupid.

"That sweet girl just turned eighteen," the conservation officer smirked. "Did you give her a very happy birthday, Caleb?"

"Look, if you're going to kill us, then kill us. I'm not answering any of your disgusting questions," Caleb seethed.

"Give them a break, Jacob," Girard finally said. "It's not polite to play with your food."

Jacob, the conservation officer, shrugged and stoked the fire. "Like to play with that rack, though."

Caleb gripped my thighs and hauled me into his lap, facing him. My "rack," beneath my Care Bear sweatshirt, ended up pressed against his chest.

Jacob barked a laugh. "You're no fun."

"Hmm. Fun," Caleb grunted, stroking the back of my neck.

Despite the situation, Caleb's soft touch was comforting. I wrapped my arms around his waist and laid my head on his shoulder.

"Aww, isn't that the cutest thing since a puddle of puppies," Girard smirked.

"Are you going to kill us?" Caleb asked.

I shuddered against him, but he was right. It was better to know than to be left in suspense.

Girard was silent for a long time. I turned my head to peek at him, and he was rubbing his chin thoughtfully.

"Caleb's a strong young man," he said slowly.

"Yeah. And?" Caleb growled.

I rubbed little circles on his lower back, trying to calm him down.

"And that means you can work for me," Girard beamed.

"I won't work for you if you kill Jacey," Caleb said flatly.

Girard let out a rolling chuckle. "I kind of figured. I'll put you up in a nice little tent, don't worry. Besides, Jacey looks young and strong, too..."

"She can't," Caleb cut in. "She can't work for you."

Girard raised an eyebrow. "Oh? And why not?"

Caleb hugged me more tightly. "Jacey is pregnant."

What? Since when?! I hazarded a look up at Caleb, but his face was unreadable.

Was he inventing a pregnancy just to get me out of hard labor?

Jacob slapped his knee again and began guffawing loudly. "You knocked up your sister?!"

"Step. Stepsister," Caleb muttered.

"Oh God, you kill me. You kill me!" Jacob gasped. "Lord, if I didn't have a pacemaker, I'd be dead right now."

"How very unfortunate," Caleb grumbled.

Girard just looked at us, his eyebrows now hitting his hairline. "You really did knock up your sister."

Caleb sighed but did not bother to correct them this time. He seemed to relax a little as I rubbed his back.

"Your parents must be so proud," Jacob wheezed.

"Yeah. Extremely," Caleb deadpanned.

"They threw you out of the house," Girard said shrewdly.

Well, they'd thrown us out of the Suburban, but that had nothing to do with them thinking Caleb had gotten me pregnant. To my knowledge, they had no idea about Caleb and me.

But Caleb kept the lie going. He began stroking the back of my neck again. "Ding, ding. We have a winner."

"Well, isn't that convenient. Doesn't seem you've got anything else going on with your life, so you might as well join the crew," Girard replied.

"We die if I say 'no,' right?" Caleb asked.

Girard laughed. "Ding, ding. We have a winner."

"Then I guess I'm a logger now," Caleb said.

"Good, glad that's out of the way. We'll be flying into a different lake tomorrow when the sun comes up," Girard informed us. "Then, we'll get you set up in our campsite."

"Lots of logging to be had everywhere around these parts," Jacob explained.

Girard nodded. "Yes. You inconvenienced us, since we had to abandon this last site, but that doesn't mean there isn't a shitton of other places to log."

"Did it ever occur to you to do, I don't know, legal logging?" Caleb asked.

"You need licenses and other bullshit for that. Just costs money," Girard snorted.

"And a criminal record doesn't help. Or being on the lam," Jacob pointed out.

Caleb twirled the baby hairs at the back of my neck. "Color me surprised."

"I didn't think you would be," Girard replied without shame. "All right, now, let's get some shuteye. Oh, and if you try to escape, we'll shoot you."

"Noted," Caleb said.

Girard settled himself against a log, tipped his head forward, and was soon snoring.

Jacob seemed to have appointed himself our overseer and just stared at us, licking his lips. "Back hole still untouched or did you rip that one, too?" he asked.

Caleb jerked and I could tell he was trying to get up, but I wrapped myself around him tightly. I didn't want him to die. With no other options, Caleb merely spat in Jacob's direction. "Fuck you!"

Jacob laughed and held up his hands. "Man, you're like a dog with a bone."

"And you're disgusting," Caleb snapped.

Jacob shrugged. "I'm authentic."

"Yeah, whatever woman said that to you just wanted you to get off and out. Prostitute?" Caleb asked sweetly.

"Caleb!" I scolded him.

Jacob's expression turned sour. "I hope you try to run. I'll shoot you and take your little filly here for myself."

"Not gonna happen," Caleb said.

I tugged on the back of Caleb's hair. "Don't sink to his level. And don't piss him off!" I hissed in his ear.

Caleb sighed and nodded.

"She's got your balls in her pocket, I see," Jacob laughed nastily.

I could hear Caleb's teeth grind against each other, but he didn't answer.

Jacob kept laughing to himself, then he settled back, got comfortable, and just watched us.

After about an hour, another problem arose. I bit my lip against it, but it was no use. "Caleb," I whispered. "I need to pee."

Caleb's eyes widened. "Shit."

"Maybe that, too," I said, embarrassed.

"Fuck." Caleb sighed. "Fuck, me, too."

"Trouble in paradise?" Jacob asked.

A chill crept up my spine. Oh God, was he the one who was going to take me to go?

"We have to go to the bathroom," Caleb said evenly. "I'm taking Jacey up to the outhouse. You can stay right here."

"So you can run off? No, don't think so. I'll take Jacey up to the outhouse," Jacob replied with a lascivious wink in my direction.

I wished right then I didn't have a bladder. "Maybe I can hold it?" I murmured, though there was an edge of desperation to my tone. I'd already held it too long.

Caleb pushed me gently off his lap and helped me stand. It was even worse standing. I crossed my legs like a little kid. I couldn't help it. "I'm taking Jacey up to the outhouse. If we try to run, you can always shoot us. But you're not going to see her in that position."

Jacob leveled his gun on us. "Really."

Caleb pushed me behind him. "Really."

"Jake," Girard muttered from where it looked like he was sleeping. "Stop being pervy and let them go to the bathroom. I don't want the plane smelling like piss." He rummaged in the bag next to him and tossed Caleb a roll of toilet paper.

Jacob lowered his weapon, his eyes flashing annoyance. "Fine. Go."

Caleb took my arm and all but dragged me with his long strides up to the outhouse. "It's okay," he murmured. "It's going to be okay. I'll guard you while you go, okay?"

Tears stung my eyes, and I tried to dash them away quickly, but Caleb saw the movement. At the outhouse, after I sat down, he sank to his knees in front of me and put his arms on my knees. "Jacey, I'm going to make it okay. And we're going to get away. Not today, probably not tomorrow, but we'll get there. You and me, we're a team in this."

I nodded. "Okay." I blushed. "But I really do have to go, Caleb."

Caleb stood and stepped to the side of the outhouse, giving me privacy while watching the path at the same time.

When I was finished, I did the same for Caleb, though it had taken some insisting on my part. He'd wanted me to park it right on his lap where he could keep an eye on me.

We walked back down to the campsite, and Girard tossed us a small bottle of hand sanitizer. "Good choice."

"Nowhere to go," Caleb retorted.

Girard lifted a shoulder. "Still a good choice."

"I was kind of hoping the outhouse would be a rockin' and I could come a knockin'," Jacob grinned.

I threaded my fingers through Caleb's right hand so he couldn't punch him. Instead, Caleb walked me back to the log where we'd been sitting and hunched down next to me, staring death at Jacob.

"You don't have much of a sense of humor," Jacob complained.

Caleb was about to retort. I knew he was. So I squeezed his hand as hard as I could.

His mouth closed.

I leaned my head against Caleb's arm, and his breathing calmed.

"You two are cuter than a bug's ear," Jacob chuckled. "Got his own sister knocked up. That's one for the ages."

"Stepsister," I said, even though it wouldn't make a difference.

Jacob waved a hand. "Semantics."

"It matters," I insisted.

"Not as much as you think," Girard said from his comfortable position.

I sighed. "I give up," I muttered to Caleb.

"Their opinion doesn't matter anyway," Caleb whispered back. "What matters is you and me."

"Get some sleep," Girard said.

Caleb snuggled me into his side and kissed my temple. "Go to sleep, Jacey. I'll keep watch."

"But..." I said.

"Go to sleep. We'll be all right. Everything is going to be okay." Caleb's reassurances lulled me to sleep. "I love you."

"I love you, too," I mumbled.

2

———————————————

THE LOGGING OPERATION

-Caleb-

The small seaplane touched down on a small lake then taxied to a dock hidden by overhanging trees.

Jacey leaned against me, pretending to sleep. I knew she was pretending because of the way she was breathing, but honestly, it was for the best. I didn't trust Jacob or Girard as far as I could throw them.

"All right, everybody off," Girard said.

Jacob waved his gun at us.

"Time to be awake, love," I whispered to Jacey.

Jacey popped her head up and started when she saw the gun.

"My other one's even bigger," Jacob grinned, grabbing his crotch.

I put myself between Jacey and Jacob as we got up, and the pilot opened the door. In short order, Girard, Jacey, and I were on the dock.

Jacob gave a little wave from inside the seaplane. "Gotta get back to work and all that. Them bodies aren't gonna disappear themselves."

Jacey shuddered, and I grimaced.

"Come on," Girard said. "Off to camp."

As we walked up a dirt path, we could hear the seaplane take off behind us.

The logging camp was spread out in the woods with a large central cook tent. All the tents were camouflage colored.

"Well, would you look who's here!" one logger said, standing up from his camp chair in front of what I assumed was his tent.

I recognized him as well. He'd been listening to Jacey and me have sex when we thought we were going to die. I scowled at him.

"Boy's made the wise decision to join the crew," Girard chuckled, and those close enough to hear laughed as well.

"Bet you made him an offer he couldn't refuse," another logger joked.

"I did, actually," Girard grinned. "Let's put up another tent, boys. More toward the center than the outside. Don't want these two getting any ideas."

A tent was soon provided, complete with air mattress and blankets. It was a queen size mattress that took up most of the tent. None of us had any illusions about sleeping arrangements.

"Dinner's at five. No food in the tent. Wouldn't want a bear to get you," Girard laughed.

Jacey dove into the tent without any prompting from me. I got in after her and zipped the door shut.

After toeing off our shoes, we sat up on the mattress next to each other, completely shell shocked.

Then Jacey sniffled, and her shoulders shook.

I gathered her in my arms and laid us both down on the mattress, tucking her in under the blankets. I wanted to say it was okay, that it was going to be okay. But both of those might turn out to be a lie.

Jacey gripped my shirt and sobbed silently into my shoulder.

I wished every one of those men dead, especially Girard and Jacob, for making her despair this way.

Jacey hooked a leg around mine, trying to get closer, and I slid a hand down to cup her bottom, holding her pressed tight to me.

That, of course, created another problem. I bit my lip, willing myself not to get erect.

"It's okay," Jacey whispered, her hand working between us to rub my hardening length. "It's okay. We'll be quiet. I need you, Caleb."

I felt as though someone had smacked me on the back of the head. I groaned, dazed, as she worked me through my pants.

"Stop, stop," I whispered back. "I want to cum inside you, not in my pants." I pushed her hand away and unzipped my jeans then hers. Then I pulled her pants and underwear down and slipped inside her.

Jacey made a needy sound in her throat that spoke right to my balls. I pushed my hand up under her shirt and pinched her sensitive nipple.

I thrust inside her, fusing my mouth over hers to capture most of the noise we made, letting the blankets covering us muffle the sounds of our bodies coming together over and over again.

Jacey came so sweetly around my cock, and I followed her over the edge, pumping my cum into her. I held her, my dick buried deep as it twitched everything my balls had been holding into her passage.

"You're cumming a lot," Jacey observed, and I agreed with a nod.

"I really need to see if Girard has condoms," I said, brushing her hair off her cheek. As I released the last drops of my semen into her, I rolled onto my back so Jacey's thighs straddled my hips.

Careful not to dislodge me from her sweet, wet heat, Jacey shed her clothes entirely and pulled my shirt over my head. Then she laid against my chest so we were skin to skin, my cock still buried deep inside her. Even though I'd ejaculated all that cum, I still had a semi. That's what this woman did to me.

"We can do it again, if you want," Jacey whispered in my ear.

I chuckled softly. "You can feel it, huh?"

"I know when it's still big like that you want more," Jacey said, blushing.

I fused my lips to Jacey's, luxuriously licking her tongue. "When I'm with you, I always want more," I replied hotly.

Jacey's blush deepened. "I noticed."

"You like it?" I murmured in her ear, anxious about her answer.

Jacey was now almost crimson. "Yeah. I like it."

"You like it a little rough?" I asked cautiously.

With a swallow, Jacey responded, "You want to give it to me a little rough?"

"This time... yeah. But I won't if you don't like it," I said quickly.

Jacey kissed me then kissed along my earlobe. "A little rough is okay."

I rolled Jacey underneath me and pinned her hands over her head, thrusting sharply inside her.

Jacey's head rolled back, and she arched, showcasing those bouncing, beautiful breasts.

I bit a rosy nipple. I had to. It was just too tempting.

With a cry, Jacey dug her nails into my back and I knew she was making track marks there.

"Yeah, babe, come for me," I grunted, redoubling my efforts. Our hips slapped together in such a way that the blankets couldn't muffle.

Jacey bit down on my lower lip to prevent herself from crying out as her passage gripped my cock. I groaned and found nirvana again.

There was clapping and cheering outside the tent, and Jacey buried her face in my neck, her whole body pink with embarrassment.

"Guess we weren't as quiet as we hoped," I grumbled. "I'm sorry."

"I asked you first," Jacey said.

I rubbed her back, tracing my fingertips down her spine. "I know. I still feel bad."

"Don't." Jacey took a deep breath, kissed my neck, then my lips.

I groaned as softly as I could. "Jacey..."

Jacey settled down then and laid a hand over my heart. "I love you. I don't care who knows it."

With a soft kiss, I murmured against her lips, "I love you, too."

WE WERE ROUSTED from sleep by someone shaking the tent as though there were a violent windstorm.

"Get up, lover boy. You missed dinner," Girard said. "You're going to want breakfast before we head off to work."

I sighed and gave Jacey a kiss.

She, in turn, wrapped her hand around my morning wood.

I took a sharp breath. "Jacey," I whispered, "there isn't time..." The rest was lost as I bit back a moan while Jacey stroked me fast up and down.

I erupted in her hand and got a little on her legs and stomach, adding to the dried cum that was already there. "I'll... see about showering facilities," I said before standing and pulling on my clothes. I caressed Jacey's cheek and pressed my forehead to hers. "I'll be back later."

"Promise?" Jacey asked worriedly.

"Promise," I replied firmly.

Then I pulled the blankets up over Jacey's chest and stepped out of the tent, quickly zipping the door shut behind me.

"What do we do about showers here?" I asked Girard once we got to breakfast. "And what does Jacey eat?"

"Jacey'll be in camp with Stumpy. He'll whip her something up," Girard said. His mouth twitched with humor as he looked at me. "Hot night?"

I grimaced. "No comment."

"Well, showers, and I'm assuming Jacey's going to need a fair few, are actually done in the lake with some soap. Though I think we can scare up some shampoo and conditioner," Girard stated.

My eye ticked. "That doesn't allow for a lot of privacy."

"It does if she goes ahead and hops in the lake midday while we're logging," Girard replied. "Then it's just her and Stumpy."

"What if I don't like Stumpy looking at my girl?" I growled.

Girard chuckled. "Stumpy's like eighty years old and he's

missing a leg. Trust me, she'd be giving him the thrill of a lifetime just to be able to watch."

I scowled at Girard. "I don't like-"

"Son, I don't care what you don't like. That's the best I can do for you. Now, get to eating," Girard barked.

I stared Girard down for a while then realized he wasn't backing down, and I had no choice. I turned and stomped in the direction of the cook tent.

When I got there, the men started making remarks about Jacey's and my sex life. I scowled over my food.

"Giving us the silent treatment, eh?" Girard asked after a while with a chuckle. He clapped me on the back. "Not going to stop them talking."

"I still really wish they would," I muttered.

"Goes with the territory, son. Eat up. You're gonna be working up quite an appetite," Girard said.

Grunting my acknowledgment, I shoveled breakfast into my mouth, not tasting a thing. Leaving Jacey alone in the campsite with some guy named Stumpy did not exactly give me warm fuzzies.

Girard handed me a pair of heavy leather gloves and had me change into steel-toed boots. Then a large tarp was pulled back to reveal a bunch of 4-wheelers.

"Hop on," Girard said, gesturing behind him.

Reluctantly, and with one last look at the tent where Jacey was waiting, I climbed onto the back of the 4-wheeler.

Everything would be okay, I tried to convince myself. Everything would be okay.

But as we drove deep into the woods in a zig-zag path that had me hopelessly lost, I began to wonder if we were ever going to get away. And if we did, where on earth would we go?

Then I stiffened my spine and pushed those thoughts away. I was going to get us out. I was.

Because I'd promised Jacey.

3

THE THRILL

-Jacey-

Once the men were gone, I heard someone hobble toward my tent. I pulled the covers closer around myself as the flap zipped open.

"Brought you some clothes, baby girl," Stumpy, or at least I assumed it was Stumpy, said. "By the sounds of last night, you're gonna need to go for a swim. So I brought a towel and some soap, too."

"Th-Thanks," I replied. "Um... would you mind giving me a little privacy to get ready for my bath?"

"Nope. Boss says I have to watch you all the time," Stumpy told me with a toothless grin.

I felt the blood drain from my face. "But then you're going to see me naked."

"I sure enough am," Stumpy smirked.

"That's not... right," I said.

"You could stay in there all covered in his cum, or you can come have a bath with me watching," Stumpy replied with a shrug.

I couldn't imagine what Caleb was going to think when I told him about this. Actually, I could, and it wasn't pretty. He might go ballistic on these people, and then we'd both get shot.

"Please?" I tried.

"Girl, you're sexy as Betty Grable. You won't give an old man a look?" Stumpy said, waggling his eyebrows.

I huffed a sigh. There was no getting out of it, I guessed. I snatched the bath pack from Stumpy, letting the blankets around me drop, then pushed past him and streaked out of the tent and down to the water.

"Lawd have mercy," I heard behind me. "LAWD have mercy. Those are the most perfect titties I've ever seen."

A blush crept over my skin, and I waded deep into the water. There were little colonies of minnows and leeches, and some surface-skipping bugs, but all of them avoided me. The leeches in this part of Canada were a thousand times more interested in fish than in people.

I went as close to a rocky outcropping as I could, thinking Stumpy couldn't see me there, and started to wash off.

Then Stumpy simply appeared on said outcropping and sat down, watching me. "You've got a nice, round, juicy bottom, too. That boy's a lucky sonofabitch."

"Uh... thanks?" I squeaked.

"You're welcome," Stumpy smiled.

I finished washing, then realized, in my haste, I'd forgotten to take the towel.

"Come back over to the dock. I've got a towel for you," Stumpy said as though reading my mind.

I waded back over to the dock, trying to imagine myself as Aphrodite rising from the water instead of plain old me because she, at least, was powerful and confident while doing it.

Stumpy held out a towel and, much to my horror, wrapped me in it instead of handing it to me. "Mmm," he murmured, sniffing me. "Strawberry."

"Eep," I replied, pulling away, yanking the towel with me.

"Careful now. Don't go falling in and hitting your head on a rock. It'd be a damn shame," Stumpy said, still ogling me.

I flitted past him and over the sandy ground back to Caleb's and my tent, zipping the door shut behind me. There was, mercifully, a change of clothes in the tent. However, I discovered there was no bra, and the T-shirt was far too tight, making me look like... well... one of Stumpy's pinup girls, I guessed. The pants also hugged my curves and were a size smaller than I would have liked.

My other clothes had disappeared.

"Uh... Stumpy?" I called.

"Yes?" the old man asked innocently.

It was then that I knew he'd done this on purpose. "I really need clothes my size."

"You really don't," Stumpy chortled. "Now, come on out and let me feed you."

I knew my breasts were a few sizes bigger than was decent to be going around without a bra, but I supposed in a camp full of men, a bra would be a tall order. But, if Stumpy had managed to scare up new panties, I didn't see why he couldn't find a bra.

I stepped out of the tent with my arms folded over my chest. "Bra," I demanded.

Stumpy smirked. "No."

I sighed. "Please?"

"Nope, now let's see the girls," Stumpy said.

I just scowled at him and kept my arms folded.

"You're hungry, aren't you?" Stumpy asked.

Shit. Now he was going to hold food over my head?

"Wouldn't want Caleb to go hungry either, now would you?" Stumpy added.

Oh God. I slowly unfolded my arms.

Stumpy stared right at my chest. It didn't escape my notice that, this tight, the shirt was also practically see-through.

"Jacket?" I asked hopefully.

Stumpy snorted. "Not a chance. All right, let's go get you some grub."

I followed Stumpy to the cook tent where he quickly whipped up some pancakes and bacon. Miserably, I sat down to eat.

"Don't you worry. We'll have you back in your tent by the time the guys get back," Stumpy said. He was watching my chest as I ate.

"That's good," I muttered.

"Otherwise they'd be on you like dogs on a steak," Stumpy continued.

And just like that, I lost my appetite. I set my knife and fork down and grimaced.

"Aww, you don't like old Stumpy's cooking?" Stumpy asked.

"I don't like old Stumpy ogling me and threatening me with a gang-bang," I grumbled.

Stumpy threw his head back and guffawed loudly. "That boy would get both of you shot if we tried it. Not that it hasn't crossed a few of our minds."

My stomach turned. "Look, Caleb is my one and only. And that's how it's going to stay."

Stumpy blinked at me. "You mean to tell me that boy's been hogging that body of yours since you became legal?"

Actually, since about the very moment I became legal, but Stumpy didn't need to know that. My cheeks flamed. "Just because I've only been with one guy..."

"Damn, damn, damn," Stumpy tsked. "Selfish boy, not letting you get out in the world and experience it. You might find better dick than his. More experienced..." Stumpy smiled suggestively at me.

I pushed my plate back and stood. "Thanks for breakfast," I said. "I'm going back to my tent now."

"Aww, hiding from old Stumpy, eh? You sure you don't want a book to read or something? Days get awfully long without something to do," Stumpy responded.

I hesitated. "Okay, I suppose a book would be good..."

"You one of them romance readers?" Stumpy asked.

I was, but I wasn't going to admit that to Stumpy. "No, fantasy or mystery. Or whatever you've got, I guess."

"Mmm, Fantasy. You're going to be featuring in a few of mine," Stumpy grinned. He took my plate and finished my food, then washed it up and put my silverware and the plate back in their respective stacks. "Come this way," he said afterward.

I followed Stumpy back to his tent but refused to go inside, which made Stumpy laugh. He came out with three battered books - one fantasy, one mystery, and, indeed, one romance. "I'm the local library," he explained.

"Okay, great," I replied, looking over the books. The romance was a bodice-ripper, I could tell by the cover. I reached for the mystery.

Stumpy held it out of my reach. "Ah, ah, ah. You've got to pay the fee."

"Fee?" I echoed.

"Give Stumpy a squeeze, and you can have the book," Stumpy said.

A squeeze? Cautiously, I opened my arms for a hug.

Stumpy chuckled, reached out, and squeezed one of my breasts instead.

I yelped and jumped back, wrapping my arms around my chest.

"Perfect. Just perfect." Stumpy handed me the book. "Enjoy. I'll be in my tent, thinking about you and jacking off."

I felt sickened and raced back to my tent with the book. I'd earned it, after all, though I was never asking Stumpy for a book again.

Once in my tent with the door zipped shut, I hugged my knees and let a few tears fall. I felt so... dirty.

I didn't even touch the book all day. My breast throbbed. It wasn't that he'd clutched it that tightly, it was that I kept reliving the memory of his skeezy touch over and over again.

As day faded into evening, I heard the four-wheelers return. I jumped when the tent door began to zip open and pushed myself as far back against the wall as I could.

When I saw it was Caleb, I let out a sob and went to him, clutching his sweaty, dirty shirt like a buoy in the middle of the ocean.

Caleb's arms went around me immediately. "What happened?" he asked.

I was about to tell him when images of him going to kill Stumpy and then getting shot for his trouble flitted across my mind. I swallowed. "N-Nothing," I cried.

Caleb pushed the rest of the way into the tent, making me fall backward onto the air mattress. He looked me over, a frown on his face.

"I-I didn't choose the outfit," I said.

"I didn't think so," Caleb responded. He looked at my chest, and I could see anger flash across his sapphire blue eyes.

"What?" I asked, looking down.

It was then that I saw the dirty paw mark of Stumpy's hand over my left breast.

"Oh... um..." I thought wildly about what I could say to calm him down.

"Who touched you?" Caleb seethed.

I swallowed. "I didn't want him to. I was just kind of... caught off guard..."

Caleb gritted his teeth. "I know, babe. I know. But no one has the right to touch you without your permission. Were you hiding in the tent all day? Were you scared?"

"A-A little," I admitted.

Caleb sat down on the mattress. I sat up so I could snuggle into him. Then he dropped his chin on top of my head. "Who?" he asked again.

"Just Stumpy. He's a dirty old man," I explained. I was trying very hard to pass it off as not a big deal.

Apparently, Caleb didn't see it that way. "He's a dead dirty old man."

I gripped Caleb's shirt. "No, please. Please, Caleb. Leave it alone. I'm so scared they'll shoot us."

"So, am I supposed to let them all paw you?" Caleb growled.

A tear rolled down my cheek. "Maybe. I don't know. I'm... I just don't want you to die."

Caleb pulled away a little bit and then kissed the tear. "Babe, I'm not going to just sit around while they hurt you."

I hiccuped. "But what other choice do we have?"

Caleb kissed me softly. "You stay right here. I'm going to have a talk with Girard."

My fingers remained tangled in his shirt. "Please don't go get shot."

Caleb untangled my fingers and kissed them one by one. "I won't. I won't, I promise."

I whimpered with fear for him as he left the tent then hugged my knees to my chest and started to pray.

4

GROUND RULES

-Caleb-

I didn't go find Stumpy, even though he was overdue for a punch in the face. I went to find Girard instead.

The men had all trundled into the cook tent and were loudly calling to Stumpy for grub. When Stumpy, standing behind the camp range, saw me enter the tent, he was suitably shaken. I guess I must have looked pretty foreboding.

Good.

I walked straight over to Girard and plunked down on the bench across from him, forcing two people to move to make space for me.

"Something on your mind, son?" Girard asked.

"Stumpy does not get to play grab-ass with my girl. None of you do. I swear, I will drown us both if it happens again. I'm not going to let her get gang-raped," I hissed.

Girard raised an eyebrow. "How did we go from Stumpy grabbing a handful to gang rape?"

"I'm telling you before we get there. I don't want there to be any ideas. None," I said firmly.

"It's hard to punish a man for his thoughts," Girard shrugged.

"How about for his actions?" I snapped.

Girard shrugged again. "He's in his eighties. How much action do you think he's going to get?"

I slammed my fist down on the plank wood table. "He doesn't get to paw my girl."

"Why not?" Girard asked.

I stared at him. "Excuse me?"

"Why not let him get a little while he's still got some lead in his pencil?" Girard continued. "She's a good-looking girl. Kind, understanding type. Think of it as charity."

My mouth hung open. "You're insane."

"And you have no choice. You're lucky I don't bring her in here now and let all the men have her for dinner," Girard sniffed.

Rage boiled up in me like I'd never felt before. Rage and desperation. "I'm not kidding. I will kill us both before I let you hurt her that way."

"I know. That's why I haven't done anything like that. Yet. You keep being a good worker, and we won't have any problems, will we?" Girard said.

By the end of this, my teeth weren't going to have any enamel left. I ground them hard. "No. No problems."

"Good. Now why don't you get your girl out here so she doesn't starve to death? Stumpy said she didn't come out for lunch," Girard told me.

"What's the cost of lunch, then, a pussy grab?" I asked bitterly.

Girard sighed. "I tell you what. You play nice, and I'll have a word with Stumpy."

I regarded Girard for a long moment, then nodded. "I'll go get Jacey." I stood from the table and went back to the tent. "It's me," I said this time before unzipping the door. From the look on her face the last time I'd come in, I'd scared her half to death.

Jacey threw her arms around me, and I held her close for a moment, breathing in her hair. She flinched when I did it.

"What?" I asked.

"No, it's not you it's just... he smelled my hair when he wrapped me up in the towel," Jacey replied looking down.

I tilted her chin up. My anger was a blazing fire threatening to get out of control, but that's not what Jacey needed. She needed my reassurances. "Listen, Girard's going to talk to Stumpy. None of that should be happening again."

"Okay." Jacey made a sound suspiciously like a sniffle, and I kissed her wet cheeks, thumbing the tears away.

I rocked Jacey for a while before informing her we had to go to dinner. "I'll be with you the whole time," I assured her.

"I know." Jacey kissed me, then threaded her fingers through mine. "Okay. Let's go."

I went first, pulling Jacey out behind me. In the setting sunlight, I could see what the men would be ogling in a few short moments, and shrugged my outer shirt off to wrap around her.

Jacey pressed her forehead to my shoulder. "Thank you."

"Anytime, love. Anytime." I brought her to the cook tent.

The looks of disappointment told me either Girard or Stumpy or both had promised a flash of nice tits. I just gave them all a triumphant smirk and brought Jacey through the food line.

Stumpy was wise enough to take a step back when I passed.

"We won't be having any more problems, will we?" I seethed at him.

"No, sir. No problems," Stumpy said quickly.

Jacey's back relaxed under my hand at those words. We took the only two side by side spaces left then started working on our hamburgers.

I could feel the stares of the men on us. Or, rather, on Jacey. I'd never considered myself to be the caveman type, but right now I wanted to beat every single one of them with a club.

"So, what do you do? Or what did you do before getting knocked up and coming here?" the logger to Jacey's left asked.

"Uh..." Jacey swallowed a bite of burger. "I was going to college."

"Bet baby put the kibosh on that plan," the logger across from her sniggered.

Jacey blushed. "Uhhh." She looked up at me.

"We're figuring it out," I said quickly. I didn't want us to get caught in the lie.

"Yeah, because you're leaving here someday, right?" someone else chuckled.

Jacey looked at me, then down at her food, then pushed it away. "I... Caleb, can we go back to the tent now?"

Wordlessly, I picked up her plate and mine. Jacey put her hand in my back pocket until I handed our plates over to Stumpy. Then I took her hand in mine and we went back to the tent.

"We're never going to get out of here, are we?" Jacey whispered once the tent door was zipped shut.

I gripped Jacey by the arms. "Don't talk like that. Of course we are. We wait. We watch. We listen. And eventually, we will get out. I promise."

I released my grip on Jacey's arms and sat down on the air mattress. Jacey curled into my lap.

"Is anyone even looking for us?" Jacey asked. "Do you think?"

"The Mounties will be. Hell, even Hank must be worried by now. We just have to get to the nearest bit of civilization and ask for help. That's all," I said.

Jacey sighed. "Oh, is that all?"

I sought Jacey's lips and kissed her. "Baby, you're my partner in this. We need to be strong and have hope. Okay?"

Jacey looked positively miserable. "I don't think I can go another day with Stumpy. I don't care what Girard said about fixing the problem."

"Fair enough," I murmured. I rubbed the back of my neck, trying to think of how we could possibly get out tonight. "I just... don't think we have enough information yet to be able to get out of here successfully. I'm sorry, Jacey."

"I would swim the lake if I had to. It was just so... awful," Jacey whispered.

I thought of the 4-wheelers. "You're sure you'd risk it? We might not make it out alive."

Jacey put a hand over her belly. Tears streamed down her cheeks. "I-I... I just can't do it again. I can't."

I nodded. "I'll see what I can do." I kissed Jacey's forehead. "Wait here."

My heart thudded in my ears as I stepped back out of the tent. I looked around carefully, trying to see where the keys to the 4-wheelers might be kept.

"Don't do it," Girard said from behind me.

I jumped.

"You'll never get away, and we will shoot you," Girard continued. He was tossing a ring of keys in his hand, taunting me.

Rage boiled up inside me. "You can't keep us here."

"I can, and I will," Girard said flatly.

I rounded on him, my hands balled into fists, prepared to punch the bastard in the face and run. "Look, you sonofa-"

There was a shriek from inside the tent.

I turned and ripped the door off the zipper, expecting to see someone had snuck in the other side.

It was worse. Much worse.

Jacey was shaking, her hands bloody. There was blood soaking up the pants they'd given her, inside her thighs and up the middle.

"I'm bleeding!" she gasped.

"Fuck," Girard muttered.

I dove into the tent. "Where are you hurt?" I asked.

"I don't know. Down there," Jacey whispered. "I-I... it's too soon for my period and this isn't..."

"This isn't period blood." I stuck my head out of the tent. "I... I think..." Realization dawned. "I think she may be losing..." God, had she really been pregnant?! "... the baby..."

Girard raised an eyebrow. "And that's a problem because...?"

"For FUCK'S sake, man, she's bleeding out!" I yelled.

Girard sighed. "Get her out of the tent. We need to take her to a doctor. Now," Girard barked.

For once, I didn't argue with him. I got out of the tent then gently lifted Jacey into my arms.

Girard pulled out a cell phone and called for a seaplane.

"Two hours," he grunted, disconnecting the call.

Two hours? I watched as Jacey's color became ashen.

"Two hours may be too late." Jacey read the truth on my face.

"Tough," Girard said. "That's the best I can do."

"I swear, if it takes me the rest of my life, I am going to kill you," I spat at Girard.

Girard shrugged. "Take a number."

It was actually Stumpy who got Jacey settled on a stretcher this time not touching her inappropriately at all. He didn't even have a lascivious comment.

I still wanted to kill him, too.

"Son, you're an in the moment kind of guy. You'll do what needs to be done. But you're not a cold-hearted killer," Girard said as though reading my mind.

"We'll find out, won't we?" I muttered.

Girard snorted. "Yeah, I suppose we will."

I held Jacey's hand, helpless to do anything else. I threaded my fingers through hers while she moaned in fear.

The seaplane arrived two-and-a-half hours later. I'd been gritting my teeth for the extra half hour, wondering where the hell it was.

"Sorry," the pilot said when we brought Jacey on the stretcher to the seaplane. "Technical difficulties, but it's all fixed n–shit, that doesn't look good."

"No shit," Girard snapped. "We need to get her to a hospital *now*."

The pilot began flicking buttons and warming up the engine.

I started to get into the plane, but Girard pulled me out. "Where do you think you're going?" he asked.

"To the hospital with Jacey," I said between my teeth.

"No can do. If I let you go, there's no reason for you two not to go wandering off ag-" Girard began.

I punched him, then reached behind him and grabbed his gun. "All right, Girard. You can tell me right now. Do you think I can shoot you?" I hissed, pointing the gun at his chest.

Girard stared at me, holding his nose, which was now dripping blood. "You're going to regret this, son."

"Not before you do. And I'm not your son," I ground out.

The pilot looked from me, to Girard, to the gun, and back again. "Um..."

"Take them to a hospital," Girard growled, even as other loggers were pulling out their guns. "Stand down, guys, I'm pretty sure the kid's prepared to do it."

Guns were holstered and I kept Girard's gun pointed at him even while I crawled into the seaplane. Then I put it to the pilot's head. "Get us to a hospital," I ordered.

The pilot didn't need to be asked twice. He taxied away from the dock and took off.

Jacey whimpered and held her stomach as we pulled up into the air. I kept the gun trained on the pilot, not daring to look back and be distracted.

"You know, Girard's not a bad guy..." the pilot tried to tell me.

"The love of my life is fucking bleeding out right now." And might be dying, I didn't add. "He's never going to get a gold star in my book."

"No, I kind of figured not. But if you could see your way to not shooting me..." the pilot gulped.

I scowled at him. "You see your way to landing us at a hospital or somewhere nearby, and I'll consider it."

The pilot nodded. He grabbed his receiver and talked to someone in French.

"What's that all about?" I asked.

"Just letting them know we're coming," the pilot said.

We landed on an airstrip that seemed to be in the middle of nowhere. I opened my mouth to protest, but the pilot quickly interrupted me. "I sent for some guys to come pick you up and take you to the hospital. I can't land just anywhere, you know."

I saw SUVs pulling up to the airstrip and decided to let it go.

When the plane stopped and the door opened, I saw a Mountie with a gun pointed right at me.

"Drop it," he said.

5

LOST AND FOUND

-Jacey-

Caleb gave his gun to the Mountie who then had him put his hands behind his back. He cuffed him and started leading him away.

"Hey!" I called weakly. "Hey, you can't do that!"

No one listened. Paramedics bustled over and picked up the stretcher, hefting me out of the seaplane and into an ambulance.

"Caleb!" I cried, reaching out as they stuck him in a different vehicle.

"Hush, dear. Worry about yourself for now," one of the paramedics said.

I shook my head. "You don't understand. He's my boyfriend. You can't take him away from me!"

"Darling..." the paramedic started to tell me.

"Jacey," I provided.

"Jacey, your boyfriend is a murderer. You're going to have to do without him for a while," the paramedic said kindly.

Murderer? "No, you've got it all wrong! What are you talking about?!" I gasped.

The paramedic patted my arm, then brought out a syringe of

something. "You're getting too agitated, Jacey. We need to calm you down."

I felt a pinch, and knew I was being injected with sedative. Aside from making me calm, it also made me drowsy.

"Caleb," I murmured as my eyelids got heavy. "Caleb... I need Caleb..."

MY EYES FELT CRUNCHY, and my body ached, but I opened my eyes just the same. "Caleb?" I mumbled, looking around. I lifted my left hand to rub away the sleep in my eyes, only to find my wrist was handcuffed to the bed.

"Oh, you're awake," a woman, Kate, who had 'RN' on her name badge said, leaning over me with a tight smile. "I'll just go get the doctor."

"Where's Caleb?" I rasped, trying to sit up.

"No, no, just lay back and rest. Here, I'll put the head of your bed up," Kate admonished me. She pressed a button on the bed and my top half sat up.

I tugged on my wrist. "Why am I handcuffed to the bed?"

The nurse blinked. "Because you're suspected of a double murder."

"Wait... what?" I asked, confused.

"Well, accomplice, actually, but still, pretty bad. Your boyfriend killed two Mounties," the nurse said in a sotto whisper.

I frowned. "That's not true."

"You can explain it all to the police, dear. Right now, I'm going to get the doctor," the nurse replied. I could tell she didn't believe me.

I tugged on my wrist again but stopped when the doctor approached.

"Hi, Jacey. How are you feeling?" the doctor asked, leaning over me.

"Trapped. Where's Caleb?" I demanded.

"Caleb Killeen is facing some serious charges. He's at the police station," the doctor said. "You're facing some pretty serious charges as well. The police would like to speak to you."

I nodded. "Good. Send them in. I'll tell them the truth."

"Uh-huh." The doctor didn't believe me, either. "Anyway, I wanted to let you know that we stopped the bleeding, but your fallopian tube was beyond repair. Luckily, you still have one good ovary and should have no trouble having children someday."

"I... was pregnant? For real?" I gaped.

"It was an ectopic pregnancy. Do you know what that means?" the doctor asked.

I shook my head.

"It means the baby was starting to grow in your fallopian tube. That's a bad place for it to grow. It was always going to end in a miscarriage. It's just lucky we were able to save your life," the doctor said.

I'd barely been pregnant, but somehow it still hurt my heart to know Caleb and I had lost a baby. I needed to tell him. "Okay. So... how long do you want to keep me?" I responded. "I need to go see Caleb."

"Jocelyn," the doctor began.

"Jacey," I corrected him.

"Jacey, you need to worry about yourself and your health for a bit," the doctor said.

I struggled in my cuffs. "I need Caleb. Nothing is going to be okay until we clear up this mess. And he deserves to know we lost the baby."

"You can ask the detective to get word to him. But right now, you need to rest," the doctor insisted. "You'll be out of here in a few days and in the custody of the Canadian police..."

"I demand to speak to the police. Right now," I said.

The doctor sighed, nodded, and walked out of the room. I heard him say, "She's ready for you now" to someone I couldn't see.

Two police officers in uniform and what I assumed was a detective in plain clothes came into my hospital room. "Ms. Jocelyn Collins?" the detective asked.

"Jacey," I replied. "You can call me Jacey."

"Jacey," the detective repeated. "I suppose you know by now that you're in some serious trouble."

I sat up on my elbows. "Where is Caleb?"

"Caleb is currently in holding," the detective said. "But I would caution you to think about yourself. Anything you say can..."

"Yes, fine, whatever. I watch TV. I have nothing to hide," I interrupted him testily. "I need to see Caleb. We've lost our baby. Please, bring him here."

The detective sighed. "I'm afraid I can't do that."

"What you're accusing him of is total bullshit!" I finally snapped. "Double murder? Girard did that! We were trying to show the Mounties where the old illegal logging camp was, and then Girard showed up and shot them!"

The detective began jotting something down on a notepad. "Girard?"

"I don't know his last name. You must have our statements and stuff from when we were rescued," I said exasperatedly.

"We do. We also have a statement from a conservation officer..." the detective began.

"Jacob? Yeah, I can tell you all about that dirty old man," I responded. "He isn't worth spit. I'll bet he pulls a runner."

The two police officers looked uncomfortable.

"What?" the detective asked.

"Jacob did take early retirement, sir," one of them mumbled.

The detective's eyebrows hit his hairline. "You're joking."

"No, sir. Said his eyes were getting bad," the other officer said.

"You don't know your ass from your elbow," I snorted.

The detective scowled at me. "Caleb Killeen was holding the weapon used to kill those Mounties when we arrested him."

"Yeah. He got it off Girard. Girard wasn't going to let him come with me to the hospital. He was basically using Caleb as slave labor, and he was going to take me in himself so I didn't do or say anything stupid," I explained.

"So... how did Mr. Killeen get Girard's gun?" the detective asked.

"He punched Girard, and he took it, and he made the pilot take us to the airstrip. Only we didn't know you were going to arrest him!" I yelled. "You should have arrested the pilot!"

The detective looked at the police officers. "We didn't arrest the pilot, did we?"

"No, sir. He gave an SOS in French..." one officer said. "We..."

"Where is he? I want him for questioning," the detective growled.

The officers swallowed. "You see, sir, he filed a false flight plan, and I don't think we got his real name..."

"So, what? You have this all tied up in a neat little bow with all these loose ends? Were you hoping I wouldn't notice your complete incompetence?!" the detective snarled.

"Well... you see, sir... we had it on very good authority... and there was the gun, sir..." one officer stuttered.

The detective's eyes narrowed. "Were Mr. Killeen's the only prints on the gun?"

"No... sir..."

"Did you run the prints?" the detective asked.

"It's still in process, sir..."

The detective shook his head. "I'm sure we'll be issuing a formal apology soon, Ms. Collins. But, in the meantime, we do need to keep Mr. Killeen in holding. He was holding the gun that shot the two Mounties."

Tears stung my eyes. "I just want him here. Can't you bring him here?"

"I'm sorry." This time, the detective did look truly sorry. "This has to be cleared up first." He patted my cuffed hand. "Get some rest. I'm sure things will look less bleak in the morning."

I turned my face away, and the detective sighed.

"Come on, you two. I'm going to be giving your whole department the dressing-down of its life," the detective said and ushered the two police officers out.

The memo that I probably wasn't a criminal did not reach the staff, however. I got some pretty painful jabs here and there and would be nearly parched before someone would bring me some water. Every time they brought me food, it was cold.

I decided it would be best just to sleep through most of this terrible experience. I didn't have any trouble doing it, either. Depression over our baby and the fact Caleb wasn't with me dug its claws into me. I cried myself to sleep every few hours, day and night.

Finally, they told me I would get to leave in police custody the next day. I'd gotten so low that I didn't really care. If I was still handcuffed to my bedrail. That must mean Caleb, too, was imprisoned. More to the point, he wasn't with me.

It was night, I thought, when I felt a hand on my left arm, removing my cuffs. I blinked my eyes open to see the detective.

"Sir...?" I mumbled.

"I need to get you out of here," the detective whispered hastily. "You're not safe."

That got my senses to sharpen. I sat up and rubbed my wrist. "I don't understand."

"This logging operation thing you stumbled upon... Girard... has his fingers in many pies and contacts at all levels of government," the detective said. "Apparently, we've been trying to nail him for years. For your own safety, you need to go into witness protection."

"Like... in America or here?" I asked.

"Here. For now. I haven't worked out all the details yet, but you need to be out of this hospital and off his radar as soon as possible," the detective stated.

"O-Okay..." I let the detective help me out of bed. I was still in my hospital gown, but the detective assured me that was a good thing as we tiptoed our way through the hospital.

We reached the alley behind the hospital. The detective used a special key so as not to set off the emergency alarm. In the alley was a black SUV with tinted windows.

I suddenly wondered if I should be trusting this man. I stopped and turned, eyeing the detective.

"You don't have a choice," the detective replied to my unspoken question.

My nostrils flared. "I'm tired of not having a choice."

"I'm sure you are," the detective said. "But I brought something to sweeten the pot." He opened the car door.

Inside, in the dome light, Caleb held out his arms to me.

I sobbed and dove into the back of the car.

"Get them out of here, Al," the detective said, thumping his hand on the top of the car before closing the back door again.

Al peeled away from the loading dock, and Caleb and I were thrown against each other. We looked out the back window just in time to see a group of black cars pull up and surround the detective.

The last thing I saw before Caleb silenced my scream was the detective getting shot and falling to the ground.

6

———

SAFE?

-Caleb-

I'd demanded to see Jacey until I was blue in the face, but the Mounties had treated me just like the killer they thought I was and threw me into holding with some very, very scary characters. One was so big and pumped up he could have snapped me like a twig. The other gave off a vibe that he'd shivved people from behind before and wasn't afraid to do it again.

Luckily, we'd all decided to remain in our own bubbles and leave each other alone. Though, I thought the Mounties had hoped Mr. Stabby would have shivved me. They were convinced I murdered the two Mounties back at the lake.

If it weren't for that detective, I'd have been screwed. I knew it.

And now, he was dead.

Jacey writhed against me, looking out the back window and screaming.

I clamped my arm around her and held her in my lap, putting my hand over her mouth. "It's over," I said. "Jacey, it's over. There's nothing we can do."

"She done screaming yet?" Al asked from the driver's seat.

I guess Al had the sensitivity of a rock. "Yes. I think so."

"Good. We've got a long way to go, and I don't like the screaming as a soundtrack for our trip," Al said.

"Where are we going?" I asked, rocking Jacey as she whimpered in my arms.

"Taking you down to the United States," Al replied.

I frowned. "That's not what the detective said..."

"Well, Dick's not here to argue, is he?" Al pointed out. "This is getting too dangerous for my taste."

"What about testifying?" I asked.

Al cranked his head around to look at me. "Caleb, right? Well, Caleb, let me tell you something. You're not testifying. Because you want to live. And you want her to live. Testifying is what the people who get caught with their hand in the cookie jar do. Innocent people forget about all this and go about their lives."

"But... those people should have to pay for what they've done..." I argued.

Al looked back at the road. "Listen, kid. You're still pure that way. Truth. Justice. The American way and all that. You think right prevails and the evil are punished and blah, blah, blah. That's not how it works in the real world. You and your girl, having a chance at the good life, that's the only justice there is to be had here. And I'm driving you down to it. Get home and stop poking the bear."

"But..." I started again.

Al turned his head. "But nothing, kid. Take care of your girl here. You've had an awful loss, and she nearly died because of this. You don't want to be involved. I'm getting you out."

An awful loss? I looked down at Jacey. "Jacey?"

Jacey sniffled. "I really was pregnant, but it happened in my fallopian tube, so that's why there was so much bleeding..."

"Oh... baby, I'm so sorry," I whispered, gathering her close and kissing her.

"But... but I can still have a baby. When we're ready." Jacey gave me a watery smile.

Still, she'd gone through hell without me. I didn't want that to happen again. I turned to Al. "All right. If they don't bother me, I won't bother them."

"Good attitude." Al fell silent then, and since I didn't have any more questions for him, so did I.

Jacey curled her fingers into my shirt, and I held her closer.

I kissed her shoulder. "I'm so sorry I wasn't there."

"They didn't give you much of a choice," Jacey replied miserably.

I cupped the back of her head, cradling her against my body. "I still wish I'd been there. You shouldn't have had to face that alone."

Jacey sniffled then swallowed the rest of her tears. "Thank you," she whispered.

"I love you," I whispered back.

Al kept his eyes on the road, but I could see him roll his eyes in the rearview mirror. He was used to a harsher kind of life, I guessed. One that was not filled with many 'I love yous.'

After a bit, Al handed back a change of clothes for Jacey, and respectfully kept his eyes forward while I helped her into them. We stopped only for gas and bathroom breaks. Jacey was still bleeding after her surgery. She assured me it was because her body was adjusting to the loss of the pregnancy. It wasn't her period, and it wasn't anything I should be alarmed about.

It didn't stop me from worrying, all the way to the border.

"I've got two Americans here I need to drop off," Al said to the border patrol as he stopped next to one of their booths in International Falls.

The border patrolman blinked and looked in the back where Jacey and I were sitting, now properly buckled up. "Drop them off?"

"Yeah. Eighteen-year-old girl, twenty-two-year-old guy. Lost their passports in Canada. I've verified them." Al then flashed some sort of badge that made the patrolman's eyes widen.

"Come on out," the patrolman said quickly to Jacey and me. We stepped out of the car, and Al gave us a single wave before turning his car around and heading back the way he came.

The patrolman brought us to a main building and had us sit down. "Did you have a plan for getting back home?" he asked.

I looked at Jacey, who was hanging on my arm. "We both lost our wallets. We don't have cab fare or anything like that. Honestly, I didn't know Al was just going to drop us here."

"Oh. Well, that makes things a bit difficult..." The patrolman frowned. "Is there anyone you can call?"

I sighed. "Not anyone's number I can remember off the top of my head. We don't have our cell phones, either."

"Dang, that sucks," the patrolman said.

"I remember a number." Jacey didn't look happy about it, though.

"Whose?" I asked.

Jacey swallowed. "Dad's."

I groaned. "Oh, FUCK no."

"What's wrong with calling her parents?" the patrolman responded. His eyes narrowed. "Is she really eighteen?"

"Yes, she's really eighteen," I said exasperatedly. "It's just... our parents don't exactly approve of us."

"Because you're older?" the patrolman asked.

I scrubbed my hand over my face. This was going to be fun. "Because they're married. My mother married her father."

"You're... brother and sister?!" the patrolman gaped.

"Not biologically," Jacey said quickly. "I was eight when my mother left. Caleb was twelve when his father got cancer. This all just... sort of... happened."

"Hmm. Can't say as I'd be happy about it if you were my kids, either, but it's not illegal," the patrolman grunted. He waved us both over to a desk then produced a phone connected to a landline. "Start dialing."

I groaned. "Is there really no other choice?"

"No," the patrolman said firmly.

Jacey lifted the handset and punched in the black numbers onto the yellow screen.

The patrolman put the call on speaker.

After a few rings, Hank picked up. "Yes?" he asked in a clipped tone. "Who is this?"

"Sir, this is border patrol. There's been a handoff of your children from the Royal Canadian Mounted Police to the United States Border Patrol. Your children don't have their passports, or their phones, or any money with them. I have reason to believe they were rescued from a dangerous situation." The patrolman eyed us both.

What kind of badge had Al been packing?!

"Are you telling me my Jacey and Caleb were doing something criminal?!" Hank shouted. "I knew it. I knew that bastard was going to get my baby into trouble..."

"Um... no, sir. In my experience, this kind of handoff only happens when good people end up in bad situations. I can't go into detail. I don't even know the details. But the kind of officer who dropped them off usually works in witness protection," the patrolman said in a low tone.

"Witness..." Hank trailed off.

"Is that Caleb? Jacey?" I could hear my mother in the background. "Are they all right? Where are they?"

Hank sighed angrily. "They're... which border crossing are they at?"

"International Falls, sir," the patrolman said.

"We'll be there in twelve hours." The line cut.

"Are you all right, Jacey? Is Caleb okay? Oh sure, Hank, we're just peachy," I grumbled.

Jacey put a hand on my chest. "At least they're coming to get us."

"I can't even imagine how much fun that car ride's going to be." I took Jacey's hand just the same and kissed her fingertips. "It'll be okay."

"I don't know about that. But at least we won't get shot. Probably," Jacey replied worriedly.

I kissed the top of her head. "Don't worry. I'm the only one who might get shot."

"Yeah, that was what I was worried about," Jacey fretted.

"Are you saying you're going into another unsafe situation?" the patrolman asked.

Jacey and I looked at each other. "Probably not?" I hazarded.

Jacey looked troubled. "Maybe this isn't such a good idea."

"No, you were right. We don't have a lot of options. And could you please stop upsetting her? She just had a miscarriage," I told the patrolman.

The patrolman gave Jacey a sad look. "Oh dear. I am so sorry. Is it because you're brother and sister?"

I rolled my eyes and escorted Jacey back to our chairs. "We're. Not. Related."

"Right, right. But what happened?" the patrolman asked.

"You're getting a bit personal here, sir..." I warned him.

Jacey patted my arm. "Ectopic pregnancy."

The patrolman tsked. "My wife had one of those. Doctor said you should wait three months before trying again."

"We're not going to try again. We weren't trying before," I said flatly. "Jacey needs to go to college, and I need to finish."

"Mm. Smart," the patrolman replied.

Jacey looked up at me, her eyes troubled. "We're not going to try again?" she whispered.

"Not now. I mean, sure, somewhere down the road I expect we will, but we need to get our feet under us first," I said, stroking her hair.

Jacey gave that some thought, then nodded. "I'll need to get on some kind of birth control. You're not exactly great with condoms."

I winced. She wasn't wrong. "Well, according to this guy, we've got three months to figure it out."

"You're not going to touch me for three months?!" Jacey protested.

"I... we'll talk to a doctor. I don't want to hurt you," I said softly.

Jacey sighed and leaned her head against my shoulder. "Caleb Killeen, sometimes I just don't understand you."

7

───────────────

SNEAKING AROUND

-Jacey-

I must have fallen asleep on Caleb, because the next thing I knew, he was jostling me awake. I blinked blearily at him, then made a sound of protest when he scooped me off of his lap and onto the chair next to him. "Caleb!"

Caleb pointed out the window, and, sure enough, my father's Suburban was pulling up. I quickly put another prudent chair between us before my father and Jeanie walked into the main building.

My father zeroed in on Caleb automatically. "I ought to take my belt to you, boy."

"I'd like to see you try," Caleb shot back.

And just like that, things were back to normal. Caleb and my father staring each other down, and Jeanie putting her hand on my father's arm to calm him.

"You're a bad influence on my daughter. I think maybe you should find your own apartment," my father growled at Caleb as he rose.

The pleather of the chair underneath me creaked as I stood as well. "He's not a bad influence, Dad. You've got a bad temper," I said loyally.

"Well, your little adventure didn't end well, did it?" my father snapped at both of us.

I thought of the almost baby and ducked my chin. "No. No, it didn't."

"Hank, let's discuss this in the car. I don't want Caleb wasting all his money on an apartment. It's a whole year he's taking off to earn money for college," Jeanie pleaded with my father.

"Maybe he should have thought of that before he corrupted my little girl!" my father groused, but let Jeanie lead him back out of the station.

I guessed we were expected to follow.

"Caleb," I said in a low tone as I fell into step next to him. "Please don't antagonize my dad. I..."

"Jacey. We are going to fuck every goddamn day right under that bastard's roof." Caleb's jewel blue eyes flashed. "I know what we agreed about revenge fucking, but that sonofabitch..."

I bit my lip. "So, no waiting three months?"

"I'll wear condoms," Caleb grunted.

I snorted. "No, you won't."

"A man can change his ways," Caleb said.

"Did... you not wear condoms with the other girls?" I hazarded. I'd been trying not to dig too deeply into his past relationships. I didn't want to get jealous.

Caleb looked down at me, then at my father and Jeanie talking outside, then crowded me out of sight next to a vending machine and kissed me thoroughly. I could feel his thick dick through my pants and moaned against his mouth.

I would have let him have me right there in front of God, the border patrol agent, and everyone, but Caleb pulled back, panting, his forehead pressed to mine. "I always wore condoms with the other girls. Always. I never once forgot. But fuck, Jacey, you make me forget my own name, much less protection."

"Then I guess I should look into an IUD," I said breathlessly.

"Yeah. Good plan." Caleb's lips lowered to mine again.

The border patrol agent cleared his throat. "Your parents are about to come looking for you. I get the impression they don't know, so you might want to stop dry humping next to the vending machines."

Caleb reluctantly stopped the drugging kisses, and I even more reluctantly let him go.

I'd just managed to get myself presentable again when the door to the main building banged open. "Well?!" my father demanded. "Are you coming?!"

"Yes, Dad. We're coming." I walked out of the main building with Caleb close behind me. I imagined he was trying to hide his hard-on.

My father got himself into the driver's seat while Caleb and I got in the back. Jeanie was already in the passenger seat.

"Can't believe I had to drive twelve hours to pick up your asses," my father grumbled, throwing the Suburban into gear. "I can't believe how irresponsible you were, Caleb. You took Jacey back into Canada? And one of the border patrolmen out here thought you'd exposed her to some kind of dangerous situation. All you had to do was drive south. South! Did you get your directions mixed up?!"

"If I tell you you're an asshole, are you going to make me get out and walk again?" Caleb countered.

Jeanie put a hand on my father's before he could reply. "Caleb. Hank drove twelve hours to come get you. And he is very concerned about what might have happened to Jacey. Please be more polite."

Caleb opened his mouth to say something I was sure would not be complementary, so I bumped my ankle against his.

He closed his mouth and turned to stare out the window, his jaw tense.

I rubbed my tennis shoe against his and he finally smiled slightly and rubbed back.

"So what exactly did you get into?" my father demanded.

Caleb flinched and I looked down at my hands. I wasn't going to tell Caleb's story and he wasn't going to tell mine, so we both just stayed silent.

"What? Cat got your tongues?" my father grunted, turning to glare at us.

"Hank, watch the road!" Jeanie gasped.

Caleb and I both snapped our attention to the front window, but Jeanie was panicking for nothing. My father was keeping the Suburban on an even course.

Still, my father turned back around, grumbling under his breath.

"I'm sure they'll tell us when they're ready," Jeanie soothed my father.

"If I find out something happened to my Jacey because of you, Caleb Killeen..." my father growled. But his voice had lost a lot of its venom.

Caleb glanced over at me and I could tell from the heat in his eyes that he needed to blow off some steam. Namely with me riding his dick.

We'd just have to address the revenge fucking thing again later. My father was being a real pill, and Caleb was doing his best to keep it together. A handjob at an obliging rest stop might not be a bad idea.

"I... need to go to the bathroom," I lied.

"Me, too," Caleb said quickly.

My father groaned, the steering wheel creaking because he gripped it so hard. "You've GOT to be kidding me. We only just left the station!"

"I need to go, too," Jeanie added softly.

That changed my father's attitude in an instant. "Of course, my precious darling. Gotta keep baby happy." He took one of Jeanie's hands and kissed it.

I kicked Caleb when he made a retching sound.

My father glared at him in the rearview mirror. "I'll remember that the next time you're kissing your girlfriend."

Considering the fact I was Caleb's girlfriend and my father would N-E-V-E-R see us kissing, that was an empty threat.

But my father didn't know that.

My father pulled off the highway and into a cute little wooded rest stop. Jeanie jumped out of the car immediately and raced for the bathrooms.

I saw the bathrooms at this rest stop were conveniently lockable little stalls around the perimeter of the building. One side was labeled 'Women's' and the other side 'Men's.'

"I'll keep the door open," Caleb whispered to me as he strode confidently toward the men's side.

I went to the women's side, then snuck around the back of the building and over to the men's. My father was walking around the Suburban, checking the tires.

Caleb tugged my arm from inside one of the stalls, then closed and locked the door behind us.

"You are a very bad boy, Mr. Killeen," I scolded him, wagging my finger.

"I know. I'm sorry," Caleb said, sounding contrite. "But I'm not going to make it twelve hours with that asshole being... an asshole."

"That asshole happens to be my dad," I reminded Caleb. But I was already unzipping his pants.

"I'm sorry about that, too," Caleb muttered. Then his breath caught as I squeezed his dick, frowning at him. "Okay, okay, I'll lay off."

"You're only getting this because my dad *won't* lay off," I told him. Then I started jerking him off.

Caleb bit back a groan and leaned back against a side wall. "Pull your shirt up. I want to cum on your tits."

I rolled my eyes and did as he asked, pulling my bra down so my breasts popped out.

Caleb reached out and rubbed my breast, paying special attention to my nipples.

"No fair. I'm going to be all wet in the car," I sighed.

"And I'm going to think about that all the way until we stop for gas and I have you riding my dick," Caleb said.

"I'm not sure we should do that until we get home." I tried to be firm.

Caleb leaned in and licked, then nipped my nipple.

I moaned. It was a losing battle.

"There's my girl." Caleb pushed me down on my knees so his cock was level with my breasts. "Make me cum, baby."

I did just that. I jerked him off until his thick, white cum jetted onto my breasts.

Caleb did groan then.

The door shook as someone banged on it. "What's going on in there?!" my father called.

I covered my mouth with my hands.

Caleb calmly went and got some paper towels and wiped his cum off my breasts and face. "I had a hard poop, did you need to know about it?! Jesus!"

"Oh." My father's foot tapped on the concrete outside the door. "Well, hurry up. I want to get back on the road."

"Yes, sir," Caleb said sarcastically.

My father walked away, grumbling about what an ungrateful little shit Caleb was.

"Gas station," I agreed when Caleb raised an eyebrow at me.

Caleb got my breasts back into the cups of my bra and twitched my sweatshirt down. "Gas station."

Caleb left the stall first, a new swagger in his step that I wanted to swat him for. When Caleb had my father distracted, and the coast was clear, I stepped out of the stall.

"Jacey, what are you doing on the men's side?" Jeanie asked.

I jumped and turned. "Oh! Jeanie, you scared me!"

"Sorry," Jeanie said. But her eyes were narrowed on me, and she didn't seem that sorry at all. "What were you doing on the men's side?"

"I didn't like any of the stalls on the women's side?" I tried.

Jeanie shook her head slowly. "I swear that's the same stall Caleb was using. What's going on, Jacey?"

"I... this is the stall next to his. Pure coincidence," I lied.

"That's not true. I know what I saw," Jeanie said, putting her hands on her hips.

I blew out a long breath and tried to think of a better lie.

"Are you two keeping secrets from us?" Jeanie asked. "About what happened in Canada?"

Wow, I wasn't even going to have to lie. "Yes."

Jeanie put a soft hand on my shoulder. "I wish you would tell us, Jacey. And don't go sneaking around bathroom stalls with Caleb anymore. People will get the wrong idea."

They'd be getting the right idea, but I wasn't going to tell Jeanie that. "O-Okay." So much for the gas station.

Jeannie nodded, satisfied, and we made our way back to the truck.

Caleb blinked when he saw his mother. I don't know what expression she gave him, but it made him pale.

When we got into the Suburban, Caleb leaned over to me and whispered, "What happened?"

"She caught me coming out of your stall," I whispered back. "She thinks we just snuck in there to talk about Canada. Keeping secrets."

Caleb looked relieved. Then that relief melted into disappointment. "No gas station?"

"No gas station," I replied with a little pout of my own.

"What are you two whispering about?" my father demanded.

We sprang apart. "Nothing!"

"Hmm. Well, that's only going to fly for so long. Sooner or later, you're going to tell me what happened in Canada. Every little detail." My father sounded confident in his edict.

Caleb bit his lip, trying not to laugh. It was funny. I was fairly certain my father would not want to hear *every* little detail.

"You think something's funny about that, son?" my father snapped.

Caleb cleared his throat. "No, sir."

"Liar. But you won't be laughing for long. Trust me," my father grunted. Then he drove us away from the rest stop.

8
____

FOUND OUT

-Caleb-

After Jacey told me my mother saw us coming out of the same bathroom stall, I watched her carefully for any signs she might be putting two and two together.

My mother gnawed her lip and kept glancing at us in the rearview mirror. This brought me to two conclusions, 1) Jacey and I were definitely not having sex when we stopped for gas, and 2) my mother did, indeed, suspect something. I was just hoping she was keeping her mind on us keeping secrets and not moving on to us... doing other things.

About every half hour, Hank would scold us about not telling him what happened in Canada. But what exactly did he want me to say? 'Yes, sir, I fucked your daughter the second she turned 18 then nearly got us both killed? Oh, and I also killed someone. And three more people died because we stumbled on an illegal logging operation.'

It would blow the top right off Hank's head.

I might not even make it past the whole 'I fucked your daughter' part before he cut me off by strangling the life out of me.

I looked at Jacey's profile, taking in her delectable, plump lips, her shapely curves, and her slight smile when she caught me staring. My heart beat double-time, and I knew there was nothing in this universe that was going to stop me from bedding, wedding, then bedding Hank's daughter.

Wedding. I searched my feelings about it. It really was too soon to start making plans like that with Jacey; it wouldn't be fair to her. But she was the first girl I'd ever been with who I could imagine standing together in front of a priest.

I'd already said we could try for a baby in the future. And I'd meant it. And I still meant it. I was all in. And I knew Jacey was, too. I just worried about her - hell, both of us - being so young.

Jacey rubbed her ankle against mine, and I looked over at her. Her understanding smile warmed my heart.

All I wanted was to take her away again, where there weren't people to judge us, and make love to her for weeks. Months. Maybe years. No other woman had ever made me this crazy and insatiable.

When we did get to the gas station, Jacey jumped out of the Suburban and started over to my side.

"Caleb, can I talk to you? In private?" my mother asked once Hank was out of the car.

I gave Jacey a subtle wave to go away and mouthed the word 'later' through the window at her curious expression.

Then I focused my attention on my mother. "What is it, Mom?"

My mother glanced at me in the rearview mirror. Then she turned in her seat to capture my gaze. "Are you being inappropriate with Jacey?"

Ah, there it was. She had worked it out. I debated lying to her, but I couldn't hold her stare and lie to her at the same time. I never could.

"That's really between Jacey and me, Mom," I said instead. I sounded annoyed in my own ears. I was.

"How... far have you gone?" My mother ignored my implied protest.

I shifted uncomfortably and pulled on my seatbelt. Suddenly, it felt as though it was strangling me.

"That far." My mother drew a sharp breath. "Oh, Caleb."

"What?" I asked. "It's not like we're brother and sister."

"But you are," my mother said sadly. "And you shouldn't have taken advantage-"

I gaped at her. "Mom! I did no such thing. How can you even believe I'd-"

My mother shook her head. "I'm not saying you raped her. I'm saying, as the older adult and a mature young man, you should have kept your hands to yourself."

"It... happened. It just happened." I sighed heavily and scrubbed my face with my hands. "Mom. It's too late now, anyway. I can't re-virginate her."

"You took that sweet young girl's virginity?!" my mother gasped.

I groaned. "Mom, can we please just leave it as something between Jacey and me?"

"No. You need to end things right now. My God, you could get her pregnant!" my mother objected.

I rubbed the back of my neck and looked away.

"Oh my God, is she PREGNANT?!" my mother shouted.

I looked outside the Suburban to see Hank pumping gas. But his head turned our way when my mother shouted. "Mom, please keep it down. And no, she's not pregnant. Anymore."

"A-Any-did-did you take her for an abortion?" my mother asked.

"No." I swallowed. "She had an ectopic pregnancy."

"Oh. Oh that poor dear." My mother glared at me. "How could you do that to that sweet little girl?"

I crossed my arms. "She's not a little girl."

"She is to Hank! Good Lord, he's going to *kill* you!" My mother paled as realization dawned.

"Mom, please don't bring Hank into this," I all but begged. I wasn't really afraid for myself. I was afraid for Jacey.

"You need to stop this right now. RIGHT now," my mother ordered me.

"I... I can't." I looked down at my hands. "I love her, Mom."

I could feel my mother's eyes like lasers on the top of my head. "You... what now?"

"I love Jacey. I love her. Not as a sister." I sighed. "I love her as a person and a full-grown woman. I'm not going to give her up."

"You... Caleb. You've been very selfish and irresponsible. I will be very, very disappointed in you if you continue to be that way," my mother stated.

"Then I guess you'll just have to go on being disappointed." This time, I looked my mother right in her eyes. "I love Jacey Collins. There's no one like her in all the world, and by some miracle she's decided she wants to be mine. I'm not leaving her unless she sends me away."

My mother's eyes welled up with tears. "Caleb, you're both being so foolish. It's... it's disgusting..."

"There is nothing disgusting about it," I said firmly, reeling from the very idea. She might as well have slapped me.

"Well, I think it's disgusting, and I will never condone it. Never." A tear rolled down my mother's cheek, but she angrily dashed it away. "However, I don't want Hank to kill you, either, so I won't say a word about it."

I wasn't sure exactly what to say to that except, "Thank you?"

"You should be thanking me," my mother huffed then turned to face front again. She wouldn't look at me, not even in the mirror.

Jacey returned with an armload of snacks. Hank must have given her money to buy some. When she got into the back of the car, my mother huffed again.

"What's wrong?" Jacey whispered, handing me a bag of my favorite chips.

"She knows," I replied.

Jacey paled.

"Oh, don't worry. I won't tell your father. I rather like my son living," my mother sniffed.

"Okay. Okay, good. Thank you, Jeanie. I-" Jacey began.

My mother whirled around. "You're making a mistake. Both of you."

Jacey shrank back, and I took her hand. "Mom..."

My mother was already staring out the windshield again.

"Mom..."

But she wouldn't answer me.

Hank got in the Suburban then and looked at the three of us. "What? What's going on?"

I quickly let go of Jacey's hand.

"The children are keeping secrets," my mother said flatly. "And I can't get them to tell us the truth."

Hank glowered at Jacey and me in the rearview mirror. "You're both selfish assholes. Upsetting your mother this way. While she's pregnant, no less!"

"Just leave it, Hank. There's no talking to them." My mother still stared out the windshield.

Hank gave an indignant snort then drove out of the gas station.

When I went to rub my ankle against Jacey's, I noted that hers was trembling. I saw her folding and refolding her hands in her lap, her teeth sunk deep into her lower lip.

My baby was trying not to cry.

I pretended I was 'manspreading' and rubbed my calf and knee against hers as well. Jacey gave me a grateful look.

My mother wouldn't talk to either one of us the whole rest of the way home. Hank took a leaf from her book and did the same.

As soon as the garage door opened, Jacey scrambled out of the Suburban. My mother wouldn't so much as glance my way as she got out.

Hank went around the Suburban and put his arm around my mother, glaring at me over his shoulder.

I rubbed my temples then went inside as well.

Jacey was not in the living room, as I'd expected.

"Selfish girl won't even stop and have a proper conversation," Hank muttered to my mother, settling them both down on the sofa. "Running off to her room."

Ah. Her room.

Good.

"Guess I'm a selfish guy, then, too," I retorted and headed to my own room.

The most annoying thing about Jacey and my rooms was that they were Jack-and-Jill style, two bedrooms connected by a shared bathroom. I had a door that opened into the bathroom, and so did she. We'd had a couple of close calls over the years, but mostly we'd managed the bathroom situation without too much awkwardness.

It was a godsend now, however. I went into my room, locked the door, then walked straight through the bathroom and into Jacey's bedroom.

Jacey was curled up on her bed, holding Cheer Bear to her chest. When she saw me, she laid Cheer Bear aside and reached for me.

I got on her queen bed with her and wrapped my arms around her while Jacey plastered herself to me. Her cheek was wet, and tears soaked through my shirt as we laid there in silence for a while.

"Are we doing something wrong, Caleb?" Jacey finally asked.

My grip on her tightened. "No. Absolutely not."

"Your mother seems to think so," Jacey whispered.

I sighed and kissed the top of her head. "My mother's got this idea of us playing 'happy families.' She's only got that one way of looking at things."

"Like that we're brother and sister?" Jacey inferred.

"Like that we're brother and sister," I agreed. "But that's not what we are, and God help me, we never were. A brother doesn't think about his sister the way I think about you."

Jacey folded her hands on my chest and tucked her chin onto them, looking down at me. "What did you think about me?"

I rubbed my hand down her body to get a nice handful of her backside. "You know what I thought about you."

"Hmm... I'm not sure..." Jacey said with false innocence.

I chuckled and threaded my fingers through her hair and pulled her mouth down to mine.

Jacey's kiss tasted salty from her tears.

"We don't need my mother's approval," I murmured against her lips. "We feel how we feel. That's it."

"That's it," Jacey echoed with a slow nod.

9

HOME STEAMY HOME

-Jacey-

Caleb, of course, wasn't satisfied with just a kiss. But then, neither was I. I straddled Caleb's hips and pulled my sweatshirt over my head.

"Mmm... yeah, baby. Just like that," Caleb said, squeezing my thighs as I ground against him.

I reached behind me and unsnapped my bra.

Caleb licked his lips. "Feed me those titties."

I giggled but did as he asked, leaning forward and curving my hand behind his head so he could lick and suck to his heart's content.

After feasting for a while, Caleb laid his head back and groaned. "Baby, we need a condom."

Oh. Right. I would have forgotten. "Where are they?" I asked.

"Sock drawer. Under the socks." Caleb gave my thighs one last squeeze before releasing me.

I went through the shared bathroom and into Caleb's room. It felt forbidden in a kind of sexy way to be in there, going through his things. I found the sock drawer quickly, as well as the box of XL condoms.

It was an open box, which meant he'd used them with another woman. I tried not to think about that fact when I brought them back into my bedroom.

Caleb had used my absence as an opportunity to take his clothes off. When he saw me, his brow furrowed. "Baby, what's wrong?"

"Nothing!" I said quickly. I ripped a condom from the pack and started opening it.

Caleb plucked it from my hands and deftly opened it with his teeth.

I swallowed and looked away, concentrating on taking my clothes off.

"You either tell me what's wrong, or we're not having sex." Caleb tipped my chin up.

"It's just... you seem really adept at this," I tried to explain. "You know, and the box was already open..."

Caleb tugged me down onto the bed next to him. He smoothed my hair off my face, his own expression serious. "Baby, I can't pretend I haven't been with other women. But I can promise I won't be with anyone but you until you get tired of me and kick me to the curb."

I blinked. "You think I'll ever do that?"

"Well... I really hope not. But you're just eighteen and..." Caleb started.

"And you're just twenty-two. I have no intention of 'kicking you to the curb.' I've wanted you and fantasized about you and loved you since the moment I laid eyes on you," I confessed.

Caleb kissed me, long and slow. "That makes me feel ten feet tall. And trust me, you featured in more than a few of my fantasies."

I brought his hand down to my breast. "Show me."

"Not yet," Caleb murmured, kissing me again. "I need you too much right now." He finished taking the condom out of the packet. I watched him roll the latex over his long, thick, leaking cock.

"You'll have to teach me how to do that," I said, stroking my hand up and down the oily, lubed surface.

"Later. I promise. Fantasies and condoms. But right now I need a slice of Jacey pie," Caleb grinned. He rolled me onto my back. "Condom's lubed but..." He ran his finger along my slit and then licked it. "Don't think lube's going to be a problem."

"Is it ever?" I breathed, widening my legs for him.

"Nope." Caleb lifted one of my knees over his hip then pushed in where he belonged.

It felt... different. Not bad different, just... different. I closed my eyes while Caleb started thrusting, his thumb...

I jumped. "Caleb, that's–"

"I know. Shh. Just let me. You know I always make you feel good," Caleb murmured.

The man was seriously wriggling his thumb into my ass!

Between that and the condom, things felt very different. But, again, not bad.

"I think I prefer your dick bare," I said after a while, squeezing my eyes shut as Caleb did something sinful BACK THERE while thrusting inside me.

"Trust me, baby, I feel the same way," Caleb assured me. He wiggled his thumb again. "How do you like it?"

I blushed. "It felt weird at first, but then... I got all tingly."

"Yeah. That's what it's supposed to feel like." Caleb kissed me then started thrusting harder and faster, moving his thumb in time with his thrusts.

I panted. I clung. I came hard, biting down on his shoulder to keep from screaming his name.

Caleb groaned, and I knew he was cumming in the condom.

It wasn't the same.

"I really need to get that IUD. Like tomorrow," I muttered.

Caleb barked out a laugh. "No argument here. But are we really just going to do it the one time because the condom's...?"

"A nuisance," I decided. "It's a nuisance, and it doesn't feel right."

Caleb pulled out of me then and peeled the nuisance off, tying it at the end and tossing it on the floor. "Remind me to put that in my garbage can. We've already got one parent breathing down our necks."

"She seemed really angry," I observed. "And... disappointed, I guess?"

"She... was," Caleb said with a wince. "But there's not a whole lot we can do about that except to stop engaging in activities like this and, well, I just don't think I have that kind of restraint."

"Jeanie doesn't like it that we're in love, does she? I mean, even if we did stop having sex, she'd still be mad about that, wouldn't she? If that's the case, I don't think it matters, honestly," I replied.

"True." Caleb slid his hand down between my legs and pushed two fingers inside. "My baby, still all ready for me." He sighed. "I'm supposed to be the responsible adult. But all I can think of is that it can't hurt to do it once or twice without a condom."

I rolled my eyes. Mostly at Caleb's comment, but also because he found just the right spot inside me, and I was gushing around his fingers. "Guess that means I have to be the responsible adult."

"Yeah." Caleb brought me to orgasm with his fingers and I whimpered.

"Okay. Okay, just for tonight. Tomorrow, I'll see if I can get the IUD put in, but for the love of God, Caleb, put your dick in me!" I begged.

Caleb tossed the condom box over the side of the bed and pulled me into his lap. He knelt on the bed while he speared me with his rigid cock, and I rode him hard and fast.

"I... don't want to pull out, baby," Caleb gasped as my inner muscles began squeezing around his cock.

"Don't. Don't pull out. Fill me up," I said, hanging on for dear life as Caleb bounced me up and down on his dick.

"Good girl," Caleb wheezed, and he came at the same time I did.

Strangely, I felt an extra thrill of danger as Caleb ejaculated inside me. Like we were doing something taboo.

"Is it weird I only feel we're doing something forbidden because I didn't wear a condom, not because our parents are married?" Caleb asked.

I giggled. "I totally feel the same way."

Caleb kissed me. "That was the right way to do it. I don't want there to be anything plastic between me and you."

"Okay," I whispered.

CALEB CAME inside me one more time before dinner. Jeanie smacked plates of rice and chicken in front of us, then sat down next to my father, her eyes sharp and accusing.

"Lying," she muttered. "Under my own roof."

Fucking. She meant fucking.

I thought we'd been pretty quiet. Maybe I was wrong.

"You did say they would tell us in their own time," my father pointed out, though he also glared at us.

"Hmm. I'm starting to doubt that," Jeanie sniffed.

Caleb stabbed his chicken with his fork and sawed at it with his knife without saying a word.

I decided to do the same.

"No 'thank you' to your mother for dinner?" my father scolded.

God, I wished we were still in my bedroom with Caleb cock deep inside me, making me feel good. "Thank you, Jeanie," I said contritely.

"Thanks, Mom," Caleb echoed me. He shoved a bite of chicken into his mouth and chewed on it angrily.

"Hmph. Not very polite, these kids. After we drove all that way to get them," my father muttered.

Caleb set his knife and fork down with a loud clang. "We found an illegal logging operation when we left you guys and crossed the lake. There, I said it. Now you can let us eat in peace."

I felt the blood drain from my face. Oh God, he was really going to tell them!

My father frowned. "An illegal logging operation?"

"Yes. And four people are dead because of it. The guy who brought us to the border said it was too dangerous for us to be in witness protection. So here we are, back home, enjoying your very gracious hospitality," Caleb growled.

"Dead?" My father looked at me. "How are they dead? What happened? Jacey, did you see some people get hurt?"

I made circles in my rice with my fork. "Yes."

"Caleb, you let Jacey see people get hurt?!" my father said accusingly.

"The first one was going to rape me," I defended Caleb quietly.

Whereas I had gone pale, my father turned bright red with rage. "Rape you?!"

"Caleb saved me. Now, can we please stop talking about it?" I whispered.

My father, of course, would not let the subject go. "How did you save her, Caleb? What happened?"

"I hit him with a rock. And he died," Caleb grunted. I put my hand on his knee under the table.

"You... Caleb, you killed someone?" Jeanie gasped.

"He didn't mean to. He just wanted to stop him," I said.

Caleb's hand slid over mine. "He had a gun. I didn't know what else to do."

For once, our parents were blessedly silent.

"So... can we stop talking about it now?" I asked.

"You said there were three others," my father pressed.

Okay, apparently we couldn't stop talking about it.

"We... brought two Mounties out to the logging site for them to investigate or make arrests or whatever they were planning to do. But it turned out that the conservation officer who brought us was in the loggers' pocket. Girard showed up and shot both the Mounties," Caleb sighed.

"Girard?" my father said.

"The leader of the loggers," I explained.

"We managed to get away," Caleb went on, glossing over the whole ectopic pregnancy thing. "Then a detective decided to help us, but he got shot, too. So his colleague brought us to the border, and now, here we are."

"Oh God, how awful." Jeanie finally looked warm and sympathetic.

"Christ." My father rubbed a hand over his face. "Well, first thing's first. We need to get you to the police..."

Caleb shook his head. "We tried that already. That's how the Mounties and the detective got killed. Al, the guy in witness protection who brought us to the border, said we should just live and let live. So we live."

"But..." My father frowned.

Jeanie squeezed his arm. "We don't want them getting killed. And like Caleb said, they already tried to do the right thing and almost got killed for it. I think... now is the time to start thinking about therapy."

"Hmph." My father regarded both of us, then gave a sage nod. "Yes. Therapy. Can't go seeing all those dead people without needing therapy. Hell, Caleb even killed someone!"

Caleb flinched at my father's words. I knew the wound was still raw.

I winced and squeezed Caleb's hand.

"And it's a good thing he did, too," Jeanie decided. "Now, let's stop pestering him about it and eat our dinner."

Caleb would need sex after dinner. I knew it. And it was the best and only therapy I could offer him. I slid my hand over to the front of his pants and rubbed him there, confirming for him what was going to happen.

Parts of Caleb relaxed, except one part that stiffened under my touch. He attacked his chicken and rice with a voracious appetite.

I finished my chicken quickly as well. Then I got up and started taking people's plates, letting Caleb settle himself down.

"Should we watch a family movie?" Jeanie suggested.

Family movie? Oh God no! "Um..."

"That sounds like a great idea, love," my father said, giving Jeanie a besotted kiss.

I looked at Caleb. Caleb looked at me.

Apparently, a good therapeutic fuck was going to have to wait.

10

UNDER THE BLANKETS

-Caleb-

There was popcorn. And candy. And soda.

But most importantly, there were blankets.

Hank and my mother snuggled up under one blanket while Jacey and I sat side-by-side underneath another. My mother decided we should watch *Snow White*.

I geared up for a long, boring movie about dwarves and princes and happily-ever-afters.

Fortunately, Jacey had other ideas. She plopped our shared bowl of popcorn in my lap then slid her hand under the blanket and slowly began unzipping my pants.

I tamped down on a gasp when she finally freed my cock.

Jacey didn't look at me once. In fact, we both stared fixedly at the TV screen while Jacey jerked me off.

My mother and Hank were all cuddly and giggly, so they weren't paying any attention. But just in case, I kept that popcorn bowl firmly in my lap.

When I finally came, I bit down hard on my lip against a shout. Fuck me, but that woman was getting really good at this.

Jacey wiped her hand on the blanket then held the side of the popcorn bowl so I could discreetly put myself back in order. I wished we could cuddle. After cumming that hard, it would have been nice.

My mother let out a long sigh, and I glanced her way, wondering if she'd seen. But she was absorbed in Hank and the movie.

"Isn't it wonderful that I have my prince." My mother smiled up at Hank.

I tried not to gag. Jacey was biting her lip to stop a laugh.

"What, nothing from the peanut gallery this time, Caleb?" Hank chortled, kissing my mother on her temple.

"Wouldn't dream of having an opinion, Hank," I replied.

Hank's eyes narrowed, then he laughed loudly. "You do have a girlfriend!"

I dug my nails into the sofa. "So, what if I do?"

"Well, you have to bring her around so I can go 'ew' every time you have a romantic moment," Hank grinned.

Oh, if he only knew. He'd be doing a lot more than saying 'ew.'

"I guess I just didn't think it was fair to keep ragging on you and Mom," I grumbled, making a point of not looking at Jacey.

"Poor Jacey." Hank clucked his tongue. "Guess you have to give up that foolish crush you had on Caleb now."

Jacey swallowed. "Um... no foolish crush here."

"Good. Because it's okay for a school girl, but a grown woman knows you shouldn't be crushing on your brother," Hank said.

I wanted to hit him. I really did. But the little needlepoints of Jacey's nails found my knee under the blanket, and it stopped me.

"Why don't I make us some more popcorn?" my mother asked suddenly. She, of course, understood why the conversation was awkward.

"Sure, love. You do that." Hank hugged my mother then gave her a little spank on the backside when she stood and started for the kitchen.

My mother giggled.

I was going to have to follow up with my mother about her opinions on Jacey and me.

"So, what's she like?" Hank prodded.

I blinked at him. "Pardon?"

"Your girl. Is she pretty? She must be pretty," Hank said.

"She's beautiful," I replied quietly.

Hank smiled fondly. "Ah, that's the face of a man who's a complete goner. How long have you two been dating?"

"We... haven't been dating very long, but I've known her for years," I responded.

"Meet her in school?" Hank asked.

"Mutual acquaintances, actually." Jacey's nails were now digging hard into my knee.

"That's nice. But you didn't go to school together?" Hank said.

I tried to think of a delicate answer to that one. "We went to different schools."

"And you're not going to the same college," Hank inferred.

"No," I confirmed. "We're not."

Hank slapped his knee. "That's why you're taking the year off! It's not just about working. You want to spend some time with your girl!"

"True," I admitted.

"Well, don't let her derail your whole education. But good for you. A good woman's hard to find." Hank smiled as my mother entered the room with more popcorn. "I'm just glad I found your mother. She's the best thing that ever happened to me."

Aside from Jacey, I wanted him to add, but he didn't. I sighed. I'm sure Hank didn't mean to be insensitive, but Jacey did wilt a bit.

I wasn't the only one who was going to need therapeutic sex.

Waiting for *Snow White* to end was agony. When my mother suggested a second movie, I stood and picked up the blanket with my cum on it, folding it carefully against me. "I think I'll turn in. I've got to follow up with my job tomorrow and see if I still have one. I was supposed to start when we got back from our trip."

"Oh. Damn, yeah. You might be getting a different job," Hank said. "But good on you for being responsible."

"Thanks." I headed for my room, wondering if Jacey was going to make herself slog through another movie.

I shouldn't have worried. I barely had my foot over the threshold of my bedroom when Jacey came up behind me and closed the door quietly with her foot. She took the blanket out of my hands and tossed it aside then pressed me back against my door and kissed me.

I fumbled for the lock and turned it, then lifted Jacey under the thighs so her legs were wrapped around my waist.

Jacey sank her fingers into my hair and kissed me desperately, our teeth clicking together. Her pelvis ground against mine.

"Baby, you know where I want to cum, and it's not in my pants," I panted.

"Take me to bed, Caleb," Jacey begged.

"You want my big dick in your tight hole?" I asked hotly.

Jacey nodded emphatically.

"Me, too." I carried her to my bed, kicking the blanket on the floor aside on the way.

I laid her down on my bed and stood between her legs, taking off my shirt, pants, and boxers. Then I grabbed her bottoms, panties and all, and yanked them off her.

"Let me see the girls," I said teasingly.

Jacey rolled her eyes. "You and my tits, I swear..."

"Match made in heaven." I grinned as she pulled her sweatshirt and bra off. I stroked my shaft as I just gazed at her, all naked and beautiful and glistening wet.

And mine.

"God, I just want to eat you up," I groaned.

Jacey looked up at me with those beautiful, green, adoring eyes of hers and I was lost. "You can have whatever you want. I'm yours."

Mine.

I trailed my hand over her cheek then down her hand and over her collarbone. Jacey shivered under my touch, and my cock strained, but I ignored it. I wanted to savor her like a fine meal.

My lips followed the path of my fingertips, my tongue swirling around a nipple while my hand moved lower over her belly.

"Caleb..." Jacey whispered in a needy tone. She reached for me.

I kissed her hands and wrapped her arms around my neck then continued my feast. Jacey was warm and wet around my two fingers when I pushed them inside her. So wet.

"Caleb," Jacey begged, grinding against my hand.

"Soon, baby. Soon." I removed my fingers and her hands slid from my shoulders as I gathered up her legs and speared her with my tongue.

Jacey gripped the sheets, her thighs tightening around my head.

I kissed her thigh. "Loosen up a bit, baby. You're going to pop my head like a grape."

Jacey blushed and then I was able to go back to tasting her. And some of me. I had cum quite a lot in her earlier.

And I was going to again.

"Caleb!" Jacey cried out when I sucked on her clit. She fisted her hand in my hair, and I chuckled against her nethers.

I did it again, and felt her body find release, her juices dripping down my chin.

When I stood, Jacey was still trembling with the aftereffects of her orgasm. I shifted her so we were both on the bed then wrapped her legs around my waist and pressed my wet mouth to hers while I pushed the head of my cock into her fluttering entrance.

Jacey arched beneath me, taking every slow inch I gave her.

"That's it, baby. Take my big dick," I murmured. She felt amazing. I marveled that every time we had sex, it just got better.

"I want your big dick," Jacey gasped, and I framed her face with my hands.

"What do I do with such a dirty little mouth?" I pushed the rest of my cock in, right to the hilt, with one sure thrust.

Jacey's eyelids fluttered. "Kiss it?" she suggested.

"Mmm. Yes, I could." I leaned down and kissed her hard, pulling back and thrusting again.

Jacey mewled with need. She wrapped herself around me entirely, pushing her pelvis up off the mattress to meet my thrusts.

"That's my baby girl." I groaned. I tried to be slow and steady. I'd intended to make this round last and last, but my Jacey was just too delectable. I couldn't hold back.

Our bodies began slapping together as we made frenzied love. I could feel my balls tighten, and I reached down to pinch Jacey's clit. "Come for me, baby. Come on my big dick."

Jacey cried out, and her inner muscles began milking me for the cum I shot into her. I groaned and pressed my forehead to hers as my body found sweet release in her passage.

Then Jacey sniffled and then let out a sob.

"Hey, baby, what's the matter?" I caught some tears on my fingers. "Did I hurt you?"

Jacey shook her head. "I'm just... I'm just so happy we're home and not... there."

Ah. The whole sum of incidents was coming crashing down on her. I wondered when it would happen to me.

I started to pull out, but Jacey's nails dug into my arms, so I inched back in and rolled us both on our sides. I stroked Jacey's back and kissed her tears. "It's okay now. Didn't I promise we'd be okay?"

Jacey nodded. "You did."

I brushed my lips over hers. "Who's my baby?"

"I-I am," Jacey hiccuped.

"Yeah, you are." I rubbed her gently, everywhere I could reach.

Jacey swallowed, her tears drying up after a while. "Do you want to watch a movie?"

Considering Jacey and I both had TVs in our rooms, it wasn't a bad proposition. We could cuddle just the way I'd wanted to during *Snow White*. "Okay. One condition."

"What condition?" Jacey asked.

I gave her a wicked smile. "I get to lay my head on your boobs."

Jacey snorted a laugh. "You really like them, don't you?"

"Very much," I replied, twiddling a nipple between my fingers.

"They're yours," Jacey reminded me. "You might as well lay on them."

"Good." I re-settled us so my cheek was on one of her breasts, and she was lying on her back. I draped an arm over her middle after handing Jacey the remote.

Jacey thought for a moment, then put on an action film.

I chuckled inwardly. As though that was going to stop me from fucking her silly tonight.

11

———

BLISS

-Jacey-

Caleb was very happy to lay on my breast, licking my nipple on occasion as we watched the movie and reaching up to worry the other one with his fingers every time my body settled down. In truth, I barely knew what we were watching because Caleb was playing with my breasts and sending delightful zings through my body.

It was when the main character wriggled into a vent when Caleb remembered he had something long and thick in another tight space. Or maybe he'd never forgotten and was just giving the two of us time to rest.

In any case, Caleb rolled onto his back and took me with him so I was sitting on top of him and straddling his hips. He was so deep when we used this position it made me pant. I was always surprised I could take all of him in.

"You're doing so good, baby." Caleb took my hands and threaded his fingers through mine. "Ride me. Make us both feel good."

Whimpering, I moved up and down on his shaft, rocking my hips. When we did this, it was just so deep, almost painfully so, and I moved carefully.

Caleb squeezed my hands, sighing happily as I rode him.

Pretty soon, I did find the right angle and pace. I brought one of Caleb's hands to my overstimulated breast and cried out as he began thumbing my nipple.

Caleb groaned and pushed his hips upward, going as deep as he could as he shot up into me, and I orgasmed around him.

I flopped forward onto his chest. Caleb wrapped his arms around me and kissed me sweetly.

"Good job, baby," he murmured.

He was finally, blessedly, soft inside me, but that didn't mean I wanted him to pull out. I snuggled against his chest and looked at the TV, laughing a little when I saw the credits rolling. "We missed the movie."

"Yeah? Well, we have better forms of entertainment," Caleb said, waggling his eyebrows at me.

I giggled, then yawned. "Oh wow, you've tired me out."

"I need to sleep so I can get up early and go to that job," Caleb replied with a nod of agreement.

"Want me to write you a note?" I teased.

"Nah. What would it say, anyway?" Caleb asked.

I grinned. "'Worker unable to come in because he was marathon drilling girlfriend.'"

"Fuck yeah," Caleb chuckled. He kissed my hair. "Want me to pull out?"

"No." I flexed my muscles to hold him inside to emphasize my point.

Caleb smiled fondly and kissed me. "I might end up fucking you awake."

"Good." I closed my eyes and laid my hand over Caleb's heart.

This. This was absolute bliss.

I'D BEEN DREAMING of Caleb, so I didn't immediately realize I wasn't dreaming when Caleb groaned in my ear.

I blinked slowly awake. Caleb was hard inside me, but he wasn't trying to ravish me. He was having another bad dream.

Sweat had broken out all over his body, and his head was thrashing back and forth.

I put my hand over his mouth just in time to catch him crying out. Luckily, I'd muffled the sound.

Caleb's eyes flew open.

I ran my fingers through his hair and gazed into his eyes in the low streetlamp glow through the window.

Caleb groaned again, and his arms tightened around me, almost in a death grip. "Jacey."

"Yeah, that's me." I kissed his nose. "I'm here. I'm here, and we're in your room, and nothing bad is happening."

A shaking hand captured one of mine and squeezed it. "Jacey. My Jacey."

"Mhm. I'm all yours," I told him.

Caleb rolled us so I was underneath him and started thrusting hard and fast. It hurt, but I let him because he needed this.

"Fuck... so... fucking... tight..." he grunted with each thrust. Caleb squeezed my breasts, and I gasped in pleasure and pain.

"Baby, you're hurting me," I finally gasped.

"I know. I'm sorry. Please, let me," Caleb moaned in my ear.

I squeezed his hand, then just held him. Soon enough, Caleb came inside me with a low groan.

Tears hit my cheek, and I realized they were his and not mine. "I'm sorry, baby."

"It's okay," I whispered, stroking his back. "Shh. It's okay. I'm here, and I let you. You had my permission."

Caleb took a deep breath. "I saw Bill again."

"I thought so." I cupped my hands around Caleb's face and kissed him softly. "He's gone. I'm here. Do what you need to do."

"I just did." Caleb kissed me back. Then he smoothed his hand over my hair. "Let me make it up to you."

I gave him a wan smile. "Okay."

Caleb pulled out, and I whimpered. "Sorry. I'm sorry, baby."

"No, it's not that. It's just..." I tried to explain.

"You don't want to lose the connection," Caleb said. "I get it. I'll put it back in just as soon as I make you feel good." He then proceeded to do sinful things with his thumb and two fingers.

He had to put his other hand over my mouth because I couldn't hold back a yowl. "That's it, baby. I know how you like it."

Caleb certainly did know I liked it. I was gushing over his hand in a very short amount of time, biting down on the crook of his neck to keep from screaming.

Taking that as an invitation, Caleb sucked on the side of my neck. Hard.

"M-Marking your territory?" I gasped.

"Damn straight." Caleb took his fingers out of me, then rolled onto his back and gently slipped his cock back in.

I was sore, but I still appreciated the closeness. I stroked my hand over Caleb's cheek. "Back to sleep?" I asked.

"I can try," Caleb sighed.

"Well, I'm here. Just in case," I reminded him.

Caleb kissed me. "I know, baby. And I thank God for that every second of every day."

I smiled and snuggled back down, stroking Caleb's chest. Soon enough, his breathing evened out. I said my own little prayer that the rest of his night would be undisturbed by nightmares.

STILL DRIPPING cum from taking care of Caleb's morning wood, I sat in pajamas at the kitchen table with Jeanie and ate my cereal. My father had gone to work, and Caleb had hurried out to see about the job he may or may not have lost.

Jeanie glanced at me over my box of cereal—several times.

"Something on your mind?" I asked.

"Did you sleep with Caleb last night?" Jeanie inquired.

I looked at her over my cereal box. "Jeanie, that's not really something you can ask. It's between Caleb and me."

"I'm asking because I... I forbid you to do that under my roof," Jeanie said firmly.

She'd obviously been working up the resolve to say this to me. So, I decided I could at least be respectful in my response. "Jeanie, it's my roof, too. And Caleb's. We're not hurting anyone, and there's no risk of us setting the house on fire, so... respectfully, I really don't see how it's any of your business."

Jeanie raised her chin. "If you do it here, I'll tell your father what you and Caleb have been up to."

I stared at her open-mouthed. "You wouldn't."

"I most certainly would. I just won't have it. You've already been pregnant once. Are you even using condoms?" Jeanie demanded.

"We... did," I said evasively.

"Oh? When?" Jeanie asked.

"Er... once. Yesterday," I admitted.

"And how many times were you intimate?" Jeanie pressed.

I blushed. "Jeanie, we can't really have this conversation..."

"A few times, I'm guessing." Jeanie folded her arms over her chest. "I'll be telling Caleb, too. None of this nonsense is going on under my roof."

I frowned. "It's not nonsense. We love each other!"

"You aren't old enough to know that," Jeanie scoffed.

"Caleb said you met his father when you were sixteen and started dating. You had him the same year. He said you loved him very much," I argued.

Jeanie rubbed her temples. "You tell your children things sometimes for their own good. The truth is we were scared teenagers who had a shotgun wedding and barely knew what to do with a baby. We got along, but we were just friends. Friends and partners for Caleb's sake. You just... you don't understand. Being as young as you are, everything feels so much more... I don't know... dramatic."

"We're not being dramatic. We love each other!" I all but shouted.

"You can't know it will last. And by the time you figure that out, you could be baby-trapped," Jeanie said.

I gaped at her. "You're saying I'd baby-trap Caleb?!"

"I'm saying he might baby-trap you. Or you might just baby-trap each other. Jacey, it is far too soon..." Jeanie continued.

"We're not thinking of having children right now. I'm getting on an IUD," I said flatly.

"But not using condoms in the meantime," Jeanie accused.

I didn't have a whole lot to say to that. "I was going to see if I could get an appointment today. If I bring you proof I've had an IUD put in, will you leave Caleb and me alone?"

Jeanie shook her head. "Not in this house."

"You'd rather we do it in a dirty gas station bathroom?" I countered.

"I'd rather you not do it at all. But I don't have control over that. I only have control over this house," Janie said.

I glared at her. "You're being unfair."

"Too bad," Jeanie replied, unmoved.

I shoved my chair back. "Fine. You try telling that to Caleb. I bet he'll have a thing or two to say."

"He probably will. But that's between me and my son," Jeanie said.

I grabbed up my bowl and stormed to the sink, dumping its contents down the garbage disposal. Then I stomped off to my room.

Caleb arrived home as the sun was going down. I'd stayed in my room all day. I heard the garage door open and Caleb's heavy footsteps on the floor.

"Mom?" I heard Caleb say. "Where's Jacey?"

The rest of the conversation was muffled until Caleb let out a loud, "Are you *shitting* me right now?!"

I smiled to myself. Caleb would take care of this.

Several minutes later, Caleb came storming into his room. I stood up from my bed and walked through the bathroom to join him. He shook his head, sat on his bed, and sulked.

"You... couldn't get her to change her mind?" I asked quietly.

"No." Caleb looked up at me. He took my hands in his. "I'm going to get an apartment."

I blinked in surprise. "But... what about the money you wanted to save for medical school?"

"I'll still save some. And the money from my father. I'm going to get an apartment near the U of M campus. I know you want to be in that Spanish immersion dorm, but I just want to be close to you," Caleb said.

"Shouldn't you be close to your job?" I asked.

"I'll get a different job. I won't make a move until I have everything nailed down," Caleb told me. Then he sighed. "But that means we can't... be together here."

I frowned. "Then... can we still sleep in the same bed?"

"Doubt it. I think Mom's going to be checking," Caleb said.

Tears stung my eyes. "But Caleb," I replied, touching his cheek, "what about your nightmares?"

Caleb put his hand over mine. "I'm going to get this all done as soon as possible. In the meantime... we'll just have to think of other places where we can be... intimate."

"This is so unfair," I whispered.

Caleb pulled me into his lap and hugged me. "I know, baby. I know it is. But we're going to work it out."

I swallowed. "When you get the apartment, maybe I can come live with you? Then your mom and my dad can't stick their noses in."

"What will we tell Hank?" Caleb asked.

"As little as possible," I said.

12

____

MOVING OUT

-Caleb-

"How is your steak, Caleb?" Hank asked as we sat outside on the deck. Hank was grilling steaks, and of course, my mother had made side dishes.

I must have looked pretty doom and gloom because Hank was frowning at me. "Steak's great," I said, trying to insert some enthusiasm into my response.

The truth was, I hadn't slept more than a couple of hours in the last week because of nightmares. I was exhausted, I wasn't getting any, and the work search wasn't fantastic. Mainly because I had to hide it from my employer, Hank, and my mother.

"Good. I'm kind of a grill master myself," Hank beamed. He cocked his head. "But you do look a bit... worn."

"Working too much?" my mother chirped.

Of course, she was happy. She was probably getting it from Hank every night. I shuddered at the thought. "No, I'm fine," I said through my teeth.

I would be fine. I would be just fine if I could have Jacey. I swore, when I got my apartment, we were having sex on every surface. And then I was going to cuddle her in bed and sleep for a year.

"Darling, it's for the best," my mother whispered when Hank's focus was back on the grill.

I ignored her. If I didn't, I was going to snap.

Jacey leaned over to pour me more lemonade, and I got a good look at her cleavage. My balls just got bluer.

She didn't mean to flash me, I knew, but with tits like hers, it was hard to find shirts other than turtlenecks that completely covered the girls. Besides, Jacey's were so nice, I would be salivating over them if she'd been wearing a heavy sweater.

My mother looked hurt that I didn't engage with her and started poking at the salad on her plate.

"Jeanie, love? What's wrong?" Hank asked my mother.

"Oh, nothing," my mother said miserably. A good actress she was not.

"Is it the baby?" Hank asked anxiously.

My stomach clenched. I wanted to hold Jacey's hand while Hank and my mother talked about the baby. We'd almost had one ourselves.

"No," my mother replied with a watery smile. "Baby is just fine."

"You should have Jacey help out more around the house," Hank grumbled, giving Jacey a sharp glare. "You work too hard."

"Jacey does quite a bit. Don't worry about it." My mother patted Hank's hand.

Hank snorted. "Clearly not enough if you're this upset."

"It's just... something between Caleb and me," my mother explained, glancing my way.

Oh hell no. She did not just sic Hank on me.

"What did you do?" Hank growled at me.

Your daughter. "Nothing," I said. "We just had an argument."

"Well, whatever it was, I'm sure your mother was right, and you were wrong. You need to learn some respect," Hank spat.

That was it. That was the moment. "I expect respect in return for respect. For instance, I'd like you to respect the fact my mother and I are having some trouble, and your nose doesn't need to be in it," I snapped.

Hank's cheeks colored with rage. "As your father..."

"You are *not* my father!" I slammed my lemonade down so hard the glass cracked.

Jacey hopped up immediately with a napkin and carefully took the glass from me. I'm sure she was afraid I'd crush it in my hand and injure myself at that point.

And I would have, too.

"Damn right, I'm your father!" Hank snarled, "And you've got Jacey waiting on you hand and foot!"

"She's just trying to help, Hank, sweetheart," my mother said.

"If you live under my roof, you will respect me, young man," Hank yelled. "And you will respect your mother."

I stood. "Then maybe I won't live under your roof."

Hank was taken aback. "Excuse me?"

"I have a job. I can afford to live on my own," I informed him.

"Oh, really? Well, good for you. I suppose you'll be paying your own tuition, too?" Hank said with false sweetness.

I ground my teeth. "My father left me enough for a year or two of medical school. I don't need your money."

My mother coughed.

Hank just laughed. "Your mother and I used that money for renovations on the house. Hope you like the new kitchen."

Jacey drew a sharp breath on my behalf.

I just stood, dumbfounded. "You... what?"

"Technically, it was our money, Caleb..." my mother started.

I rounded on her. "Dad intended for that money to go toward my education!"

"Well, with Hank paying your way, I thought..." my mother explained.

"Save it. Fuck it. I'm leaving. I'll couch surf if I have to." I kicked my chair out from behind me and picked up my plate, storming toward the kitchen.

"Caleb!" Hank called imperiously. "Don't make decisions you can't take back!"

Jacey followed me into the kitchen. "Caleb, what are you going to do?"

"Baby, I'm going to get an apartment, like I said, and a new job. I'll stay with a friend for a while. You can come visit." I made sure Hank was busy arguing with my mother, then kissed Jacey swiftly on the lips. "This won't go on for long. I promise."

"Okay," Jacey whispered.

Then I went to my room and gathered up my things. I slung my pack over my shoulder and went to stand outside the sliding glass door. "Jacey, I hope to see you soon. I'll call you. Mom, Hank, fuck you very much."

"Caleb!" my mother wailed as I made my way to the garage.

"Boy, you will never get another red cent from me," Hank informed me. "Think about what you're doing."

I rounded on him. "Like I said, I'm not your son." I glanced past him to Jacey who looked stricken.

"Bye, Jacey," I said past a sudden lump in my throat. I tossed my bag in the Prius and smacked the garage door opener.

"You'll regret this," Hank hissed.

"Probably not," I retorted. Then I backed out and sped away from that house.

And my Jacey.

WILLIAM GREGORY MCMILLAN MASTERSON III was a friend I'd made at Stanford. I was most of the reason he passed the pre-med program. So, when I showed up on the doorstep of his family mansion in Mankato, he was more than happy to let me in.

"You shouldn't have gone home in the first place," Will told me as the housekeeper set me up in a guest room. "Hank always was a hothead and an asshole."

"You've never met him," I pointed out.

Will shrugged. "I didn't have to. You told enough stories."

"Well, I thought I could handle it, I guess," I grumbled. I followed him out to the pool, and Will and I sat side by side on a pair of lounges.

"You should have stayed in California and gotten a job," Will continued.

I inclined my head, almost agreeing with him. But then... "I've got a girl."

"Oh! That changes things. She from around here?" Will asked.

Delicately, I cleared my throat. "She's Hank's daughter."

"She... she's what now?" Will gaped.

"It's Hank's daughter, Jacey. Jocelyn Collins," I clarified.

"No way. No way you're screwing the daughter of the guy who's screwing you over. That's, like, poetic, man," Will laughed.

I grunted. "I guess. But it's not really like that. I really like her. I love her."

Will turned and looked at me. "Woah, man, that's something. And I mean, even better. Just think how his brain's going to explode when you marry her someday or some shit."

"Already got her pregnant," I said softly.

Will's eyes nearly bulged out of his head. "You... but you're like Mr. Condom."

"I wasn't when we were up North. Nah, man, we lost the pregnancy, and we're going to be more careful now," I replied. "I mean, she's only eighteen."

"And you banged her the second that mileage rolled over, didn't you?" Will grinned.

I rubbed the back of my neck, feeling my cheeks flush. "Maybe."

"Happy birthday to Jacey," Will whistled. "Can't wait to meet her. She must really be something to make you forget to wrap the package."

"She really is," I murmured. "I'm just hoping she can make it over here. Hank is overbearing as fuck. Which reminds me." I took out my phone.

"Aww, you're gonna call her. That's sweet," Will said, batting his eyelashes.

I grimaced. "Shut up, dickhead. You just wish you had a girl like her." I found Jacey's number in my recent calls and pressed it.

"You got me there," Will responded wistfully.

The phone rang a few times, which was unlike Jacey and me, so it didn't surprise me when Hank answered the line.

"Where the fuck are you?! Your mother is worried sick!" Hank bellowed.

'D-A-M-N!' Will mouthed from the sidelines.

"I'm at a friend's," I replied. "And last time I checked, this was Jacey's phone."

"You've got no business talking to my daughter. If you're a part of this family, you're a part of this family. If you're not, you're not. It's that simple. Now get your ass home," Hank growled.

I ground my teeth. "I'm not going back."

"Well then, there's no need to talk to Jacey, is there?" Hank said. "You two might have gotten close over that crap in Canada, but I forbid you to be friends. You hear me? I won't let you give my little girl ideas."

"Like... being independent and self-sufficient?" I asked sweetly.

Hank snorted. "You've got some cheek. If you're so worried about Jacey, you should come home."

"No can do. But give Mom my love," I said. I disconnected the call and frowned, tapping the phone against my chin thoughtfully.

"So, now you're kind of fucked, aren't you," Will voiced my thoughts. "I mean as far as seeing your girl."

"Mhm." I sighed. "Fuck."

Will sat up and swung his feet to the ground. "Well, nothing to do but come up with a plan."

"A plan?" I repeated.

"Heck yeah. Maybe we sneak her out her window in the middle of the night. Or stake out someplace she goes. Do you know where she goes? Does she have a job or something?" Will asked.

"She doesn't have a job, and Hank keeps a pretty close watch on her. No wild parties. Nothing like that," I said.

"Dude, if she didn't start fucking you, she would have ended up in a Girls Gone Nuts video," Will replied. "I've seen it. Good girl finally out from under Daddy's thumb..."

I shook my head. "Jacey's super grown up for her age. She's kind of past the whole flashing-your-boobs thing."

"Except for you," Will winked.

I chuckled. "True." I wracked my brain to think of a way I could see Jacey. And perhaps kidnap her.

"Does your stepfather's house have security?" Will asked.

"Hank has a gun," I grumbled.

"That sucks." Will stared off into space, also putting his mind to the situation. "You don't want to have to wait until she goes to college. That's another two months."

"It is." Two months. Jesus, I was going to go crazy from insomnia, and my balls were going to turn black and die.

Not to mention my heart breaking and me becoming a pining mess.

"Guess we just have to stake out the house," Will decided. "We'll use one of my cars. I'll bet Hank would recognize yours."

"And he works during the day..." I nodded. "Yeah, that plan could actually work."

"Good. Because I want to know if she has friends," Will teased.

"Ha-ha."

13

BREAKING OUT

-Jacey-

"You're telling me you don't know where he is?!" my father demanded.

I sat on the edge of my bed, looking down at the comforter. Caleb was gone. He'd tried to call, and my father had snatched the phone away. Now, my father had my phone, and I had no idea where Caleb could be. "I don't know his friends, Dad."

My father leaned in. "You'd better not be lying to me."

"I'm not! Maybe if you let me have my phone, I can find out where he is!" I argued.

"Not a chance. You'll probably run off with him to his apartment," my father scoffed.

Well, yeah, that was kind of the idea. "No, I won't," I lied.

"Jacey, you've always been a bad liar," my father said. "Now you sit right here and reflect on how disrespectful you've been to me and your mother."

"Jeanie is not my mother," I muttered before I could stop myself.

My father stabbed his finger in his face. "I am tired of the two of you trying to rip this family apart."

"We're not trying to rip the family apart!" I insisted.

"Well, you're doing a good job of it anyway. Now you sit here and reflect," my father said.

"I'm eighteen, Dad. You can't just lock me away!" I protested.

"Watch me." My father went to the door and took the skeleton key out. Then he shut it and locked it from the other side.

I raced to Caleb's room, but it was already too late. My father took Caleb's key and locked his door as well.

"Sonofabitch," I whispered to myself. I went back and sat on my bed, hugging Cheer Bear to my chest.

All I could think about was Caleb. I was so worried he'd ended up out on the streets.

I was also worried about his nightmares. I'd wanted to crawl in his bed with him so many times, but had to refrain. Stupid Jeanie.

Speaking of whom, there was a soft knock on my door a few hours later. "Jacey?"

"What?" I glared at the door.

"Your father and I were hoping you'd come out for supper," Jeanie said.

"Are you going to let me out?" I asked, trying not to get my hopes up.

The door lock slowly began to click open.

When Jeanie opened the door, I rushed at her and pushed her aside. She gasped in surprise and protectively held her belly, even though I didn't push her that hard.

Still, I used the confusion to run for the front door.

"Jacey?" my father called.

"Hank, she's trying to run away!" Jeanie yelled.

My father appeared and ran at me, grabbing my arm as I opened the front door. "Not so fast, young lady!"

Panicked, I tried to pull away from him, but my father had superior strength. His fingers dug into my arm. I knew it would leave a bruise.

"Let me go!" I shouted. "Let me go!"

"Young lady, I've had just about enough of this nonsense," my father snapped. "Now you get back in your room and..."

Jeanie wandered in, looking dazed.

My father did not release his grip on me but turned to Jeanie just the same while I struggled. "What's wrong, love?"

"She... pushed me," Jeanie said, stunned.

"She... while you're pregnant?!" my father gaped.

Jeanie just nodded mutely.

My father turned back to me, his expression darker than I'd ever seen. "How dare you. How DARE you hurt your stepmother and risk our baby!"

"I didn't–" I began.

I didn't see the punch coming.

All I remembered was hearing, "Hank, no!"

WHEN I WOKE UP, it was dark. Jeanie was sitting next to my bed, and there was a cool rag on my cheek.

"Oh, there you are," Jeanie said, sounding relieved. "I was beginning to worry."

I slapped her hand away. The rag fell to the floor with a soft, wet plop.

Jeanie winced. "I'm sorry–your father's sorry–"

"Get out," I interrupted her, my voice dripping venom.

"Jacey..."

"OUT!" I shouted.

Jeanie paled and rose from the desk chair she'd pulled up next to my bed. "I'll check on you later," she said softly then slipped out of my room and closed and locked the door.

I sat up and winced, my head spinning. When I finally righted myself, I went into the bathroom to survey the damage.

In the harsh light of the bathroom, I saw my cheek was split wide open on my cheekbone.

My hands balled into fists. I'd lost consciousness and those bastards hadn't even bothered to take me to the hospital!

I tried touching the spot with my fingertips, but it stung something terrible and continued to throb when I pulled my hand away.

Maybe it would scar.

My breathing hitched. My father had been angry. My father had been livid. But he'd never hit me before.

Every bit of him I'd held up on a pedestal crumbled and fell away. My father was a Class A sonofabitch.

I tried very hard not to cry. Very, very hard. The tears would only sting the wound.

But they came anyway, and I quickly held a Kleenex under my right eye to catch the tears that threatened to spill down my cheek.

Then a tapping sound came from my room. Not wood, but glass.

I wondered if it had started storming outside, and it was hailing, but I went to check out the noise just the same.

There was Caleb.

I undid the locks on my window and cranked it open. "Caleb!"

Caleb took one look at me and a scowl descended over his face. "What happened?"

"I tried to get away," I explained.

"And?" Caleb prompted.

With a sniffle, I looked down at the windowsill. "Dad punched me."

Caleb turned white with anger. "I'm going to kill him."

"No, please, Caleb. Let's just go. Please, get me out of here," I begged.

"That's where I come in," another man said, coming to stand next to Caleb.

"Who are you?" I asked.

"Caleb's friend, Will." Will flicked open a Swiss Army knife and began cutting the screen.

I tugged the crank on the window, even though I knew it wouldn't open far enough for me to get through. "It's no use trying to get me out this way. Even with the screen off, the window still doesn't open far en-"

Caleb kicked the screen in once Will sliced it open then kicked the window frame. It made a godawful crashing sound and the glass shattered, but it did crack right off its hinges and leave space enough for me to get out.

Unfortunately, I was sure it also alerted my father.

I glanced nervously at my door.

"Come on, baby," Caleb said, holding out his arms.

I carefully tiptoed around the glass and broken wood, then crawled through the screen and dropped into Caleb's arms.

The door rattled behind me, and I glanced up in fear.

"Let's go," Will hissed. "Escape now, murder later."

Caleb glowered at my bedroom window for a moment, but just as my father came bursting into the room, he set me down and took my hand.

And we ran.

We ran straight to a black Hummer, and Will jumped into the front seat while Caleb launched us into the back.

My father was just coming out of the house with his gun when Will hit the accelerator and we drove away.

"Hospital?" Will asked after we were about a mile away from my house.

"Yeah," Caleb said. "We've got to get her stitched up."

I winced at the idea, but Caleb was probably right.

Caleb pulled me into his lap and held me close. "Jacey. Jesus."

"He hit me. He's never hit me before. I don't... I don't even know what to think," I whispered to Caleb.

"He's an asshole. That's all you need to think. In fact, let's take thinking off the table altogether and just get you healed up, okay?" Caleb kissed me carefully and held me as though I were made of spun glass.

I curled into him and sobbed, even though it stung.

"Baby... baby, I love you. I'm gonna take care of you," Caleb murmured soothingly, stroking my hair.

Will deftly navigated us onto a highway.

"I thought we were going to the hospital?" I asked.

"We are. In the cities. Lord only knows what happens in a small town hospital. They might hand you right back over to your father," Will pointed out.

"Good thinking," Caleb said.

The trip up to the cities only took half an hour. Will dropped us off at the front doors of Urgent Care and then went to park the Hummer.

Caleb helped me navigate the process of requesting services without insurance or identification.

We were sitting in the waiting area, Will regaling me with stories of Caleb's Stanford shenanigans when the police showed up.

They went to the front desk, and the attendant pointed our way.

"Oh God..." I whispered. "Do you think it's Dad?"

"I think Hank's the type who would have come in person, but let's see," Caleb said calmly.

The policemen walked over to us. I gripped Caleb's hand.

"Ma'am," one of the officers began. "We were told you were the victim of an assault."

An assault? I looked at Caleb.

"Well, yeah," Caleb replied for me. "Her dad punched her in the face."

"I'd like to hear that from you, please," the officer said, turning to me.

I swallowed. "Yes. My father punched me in the face."

"I see." The officer made notes on a pad. "Would you mind telling me the circumstances?"

"Um..." I chewed my lower lip. I suddenly worried I was going to get my father in trouble.

"Go on," Caleb encouraged me, squeezing my hand. "I'm right here."

I took a deep breath. "I was trying to get out. My father... locked me in my room."

The officer stared up at me. "It says here you're eighteen."

"I am, Officer," I responded.

"And your father locked you up against your will?" the officer asked.

"Y-Yes..." I looked at the pad where the officer was making notes. "I tried to get away, and I pushed my stepmom, and it made my father angry–she's pregnant, you see. I didn't push her hard. I wouldn't hurt her or anything. She just happened to be between me and the door."

The officer grimaced. "So your father became angry."

"Very," I said.

"And that's when he punched you," the officer continued.

"Yes, officer, that's when he punched me. When Jeanie told him I pushed her," I replied.

"Does she need a lawyer or something?" Will asked, frowning at the officers.

The officer taking notes and asking the questions shook his head. "No. But Hank Collins might."

"What? Why?" I glanced from one officer to the other.

"Assault and false imprisonment," the officer said. "To start." He looked at me. "Would you like to press charges?"

14

GETTING MY BABY BACK

-Caleb-

"Do you want to press charges?"

Jacey's hand gripped mine as the police officer spoke. "I..." she mumbled. She looked at me. "I..."

"I'll support whatever decision you make, baby," I said, trying to sooth her by rubbing her hand with my thumb.

"Keeping in mind your father's about to have another kid he might decide to knock around someday." The second officer, who had not yet spoken, put in his two cents.

The first officer glared at his partner. "Not that we would try to sway you either way."

Jacey took a deep breath. "No. He's right. I owe it to our sibling. I'll–I'll press charges."

I kissed Jacey's temple. "That's a very brave decision."

"It is. We'll have the doctor take pictures of your wound and send us a full report," the first officer said. "The district attorney's office will be in touch, but if you ever have any questions, here's my card." The first officer handed Jacey a business card.

"Thanks," Jacey replied softly. She hunted around for someplace to put it, since she was wearing leggings.

I plucked it from her hand and stuck it in the back pocket of my jeans.

"Will you be staying with your boyfriend?" the first officer asked.

"Yes?" Jacey looked at Will.

"Absolutely," Will said. Then he rattled off his address.

The officer added it to his notes. "Thank you for your time, Miss Collins. You should hear from either me or the district attorney's office soon."

"Thank you," I replied, and the officers walked back out of Urgent Care.

Jacey leaned her head on my shoulder. I kissed the top of her head and kept holding her hand as we waited.

"Dad's going to be really angry," Jacey said softly after a while.

"It's his fault. He can be angry all he wants, but it was his fuck-up," I murmured.

"Damn straight," Will added.

Jacey raised her head. "I'm not ruining their lives, am I?"

I shrugged. "I don't know. But it's Hank who did the ruining, not you. And... like you said. We have a sibling on the way who might need protecting."

"Okay." Jacey settled her head back down on my shoulder.

"I'm here. I'm going to be here, all the way," I whispered.

Jacey looked up at me and smiled. "I know."

"Jocelyn?" a nurse called.

"I'll wait out here," Will said as Jacey and I got up. "Tell me how it goes."

I nodded and walked with Jacey over to the nurse.

The nurse looked me up and down. "Jocelyn, is it all right with you that this young man is present during your exam?"

"Yes," Jacey replied. "And please, call me Jacey."

"Jacey. It's nice to meet you." The nurse smiled in a businesslike manner then escorted us to a room.

Where we waited again.

Finally, a doctor walked in with an assistant. "Hello, I'm Dr. Elizabeth Roe. This is my assistant, Marcus. You must be Jacey and...?"

"Caleb," I provided.

"Caleb. Nice to meet you both. Oh dear, let's have a look at that cheek. Marcus, take pictures for the police, please," Dr. Roe said.

Marcus nodded and then began taking pictures, quietly asking Jacey to turn this way and that. Then he gave a thumbs-up to Dr. Roe.

Dr. Roe had Jacey sit on the exam bed then, and she took a good look at Jacey's wound. "This is going to need stitches. I'll use the absorbable kind, that way you won't have to come back here."

"Will it scar?" Jacey asked.

"I can't say for sure. But probably not," Dr. Roe replied.

"Okay." Jacey glanced at me.

As though I'd care. "Jacey, a scar won't scare me off."

Jacey relaxed.

I decided we were going to have to have a talk about this later. I felt a bit wounded that Jacey thought I'd be that superficial.

"Marcus, can you please bring the tray over—thank you," Dr. Roe said. "Now, sit as still as possible. I'm going to numb the area, so I doubt you'll feel anything more than some pulling here and there."

"Okay," Jacey responded. "Thank you."

Dr. Roe smiled and silently got to work.

Soon enough, Jacey and I were walking back out of Urgent Care with Will. Will went to get the Hummer and picked us up again at the entrance.

"Lookin' good, Jacey," Will piped up from the front seat as I got her settled and buckled up.

"Thanks," Jacey said, blushing.

"This one's mine, Will," I teased. "Go get your own smart, kind, incredibly hot chick."

"That's why I was wondering if she had friends," Will replied.

Jacey's smile faded. "I... actually really don't. My father..."

My stomach clenched. Just another reason for me to hate the man. I kissed Jacey's forehead. "You and me, we're going to have lots of friends."

"Good." Jacey kissed me suddenly.

I kissed her back, then she deepened the kiss, and I was lost until the car behind us honked its horn.

We laughed as we broke apart.

"Man, I need to get me one of you," Will sighed.

I hopped in my side of the back seat, and Will took off, the car behind us honking again.

"Jacey... were you really worried I wouldn't want you anymore if you had a scar?" I asked as Will headed for Mankato.

"Well... I..." Jacey looked down at our joined hands.

"Would it matter to you if I had a scar?" I inquired.

"No!" Jacey said immediately. "No, not at all! You could be totally covered in scars, and I'd still love you to pieces."

I kissed Jacey's hand. "That's how I feel about you. Please don't doubt that. Ever." My voice hitched while I said it.

Jacey looked stricken. "I'm sorry, Caleb. I was just self-conscious there for a bit. I never should have thought, even for a second..."

I caressed her wounded cheek, careful to avoid the stitches. "No, you shouldn't have." I leaned in and kissed her.

It was a kiss that promised so much more, and my dick strained in my pants. It had been too long. Far too long.

By the time we broke apart, both of us were panting.

"So... I kind of think I should tell the housekeeper to leave power bars, energy drinks, and condoms in your room and just leave you alone for like a week," Will chuckled from the front seat.

He wasn't wrong. "No on the condoms," I replied. "Jacey, did you...?"

"I got an IUD placed. It wasn't exactly a comfortable process, but it's in there," Jacey said.

"Good." I leaned my head back on the seat and just stared at Jacey, relieved she was with me and all in one piece.

When we got to Will's, I trotted around the side of the Hummer before Jacey could get out and tossed her over my shoulder caveman style.

Jacey shrieked with laughter. "What on earth do you think you're doing?!"

"He's taking you to his cave to have marathon sex," Will chuckled.

"That's absolutely right," I said and carried Jacey into the house.

The housekeeper, a very serious woman, blinked at Jacey and me. Her lips twitched as though she were holding back a smile.

"Power bars and energy drinks, Martha. Don't bother with condoms," Will said without missing a beat.

"Will!" Jacey gasped, scandalized.

"As you wish." Martha made a choking noise as though trying not to laugh.

Efficient as ever, by the time I got Jacey to my bedroom, there were two six-packs of energy drinks and a plate piled high with power bars, stacked in a pretty pyramid.

"See you in a few days!" Will called as I closed and locked the door.

I put Jacey down, slowly, so her body rubbed full length against mine. Jacey whined with need. We couldn't get our clothes off fast enough.

Jacey scooted up on the bed and spread her legs for me.

I leaned over her on my side and pressed my palm down over her belly. "I'm going to fill you up, baby."

"Yes, Caleb," Jacey gasped as I pushed my fingers inside her. "Fill me up. It's been so long..."

She was tight. Too tight. It'd been too long since I'd loosened her up. "Give me a few minutes, baby. I need to get you ready."

"I'm not ready?" Jacey whimpered.

"Not for my dick, no." I prowled down her body and tossed her legs over my shoulders. I licked along her delicious seam.

Jacey bucked her hips, but I held her down so I could invade her with my tongue.

"Oh God, Caleb..." Jacey moaned, fisting her hand in my hair.

I grinned and sucked on her clit. Everything about her tasted divine.

"Caleb..." Jacey gasped. "Don't stop. Please. Please don't stop."

Well, since she'd asked so politely... I started darting my tongue in and out of her, just the way I was going to do with my cock.

Jacey sobbed and came against my face, gushing her sweet juices.

I licked them all up. But I wasn't finished. My baby was still too tight. I moved back up her body and kissed her thoroughly so she could taste herself on my lips. While we kissed, I teased my fingers back up inside her and began working her hard, stretching her for my dick. "Spread your legs a little more for me... that's it. That's my good girl."

Jacey clung to me, her canal fluttering around my invading fingers. When I managed to work in a third finger, I knew she was ready.

I still didn't stop until she came, though, thumbing her clit while I finger-fucked her.

With a cry, Jacey came, clamping down around my fingers.

When she finished, I slipped my fingers out and pushed my straining dick in.

We both groaned, Jacey's body arching into mine. She was still a bit too tight, but I'd work that out with a few good thrusts.

"You're gonna be sore, baby," I warned her, holding her to me.

Jacey's response was to wrap her legs around my waist. "Then make me sore," she whispered.

I didn't need more permission than that. I started thrusting hard, but slowly, letting her body adjust. She was so wet for me, so desperate for it. Hell, I was desperate for it. I kept the slow pace until I couldn't anymore, but I thumbed her clit to force another strong orgasm out of her before I poured my cum into her.

Stars. I literally saw stars. That was how long it had been.

Jacey sobbed and held me tightly, her whole body shaking. I was shaking, too.

"Keep going," she begged, even though I knew she must be tired. "Don't stop."

I had no intention of stopping. I was going to fuck this woman silly.

"Baby, I love you," I told her as I geared up to have her again.

"I love you, too." Jacey sought my mouth and kissed me. "I love you, too."

15

GIVE AND TAKE

-Jacey-

We soaked the bed with sweat and cum and my lubricating juices. Absolutely soaked it. And still, Caleb couldn't get enough.

When I thought I couldn't move ever again, he fed me power bars. He gave me energy drinks by transferring the liquid from his mouth to mine. I felt like a baby bird.

Most of the time, Caleb's cock was inside me, whether we were actively having sex or not. I had to say I liked it. I liked all of it.

And oh my God, the positions. I thought Caleb was knowledgeable before, but he had me so many, many ways I had to elevate his experience to expert level. I'd bent and stretched in ways I'd never imagined and learned I had muscles in places I never knew about.

I didn't know day from night. Occasionally, I'd glance at the window, but Will's house had blackout blinds, so it wasn't always easy to tell if there was any sun shining in or not. But it felt like nightfall on the second or third day when Caleb finally laid down for more than just a couple of hours' rest.

Of course, I was splayed over him and had his dick inside me. I lazily stroked him while he slept, hoping to keep the nightmares at bay.

The man must have slept for twelve hours straight. I knew because I fell asleep and woke up all while he was still sleeping.

My poor baby. Jeanie was such an asshole for not letting us sleep together. He always slept easier cock deep in me.

Caleb finally blinked awake, his eyes slitted and groggy. I caressed the stubble on his cheek. "Hello, love."

"Hey, baby," Caleb yawned. "Jesus, how long was I asleep?"

"A long time. But you needed it." He was swollen inside me, and I knew what he wanted even before he rolled me underneath him.

Caleb kissed me softly and started to move. We didn't even ask permission anymore. We didn't need to. The answer was always 'yes.'

I was so sore, and after the long break, my insides throbbed in protest. But they soon got on board with the rest of me as Caleb expertly worked my body to orgasm.

"Mmm. My baby," Caleb sighed as he came inside me again.

I ran my fingers through his hair. "Can we stay like this forever?"

"I sure hope so," Caleb smiled. He kissed me softly.

I kissed him back in a slow, unhurried manner.

Caleb smiled against my lips. "Baby," he asked, twirling a lock of my hair between his fingers. "Are you really sore?"

I pouted a little and nodded.

"Let's get in a hot bath." Caleb gently pulled out of me.

I whimpered at the loss and the sore feeling when he pulled out.

"Oh, my sweet baby, you should have said something," Caleb mumbled, looking down between my legs.

I sat up and saw a little pink streak on the sheets. "It's okay. I wanted you so badly, Caleb."

"Well, let's do that bath." Caleb tried getting me to stand, but I wobbled and fell against him. So he scooped me up in his arms and carried me to the en suite bathroom.

In the bathtub, Caleb washed me tenderly, kissing the back of my neck as I sat between his legs. He even carefully washed me intimately, and I kissed his neck to hide my embarrassment.

Caleb chuckled. I must have gone pink or something because he said, "I finger-fuck you all the time, but washing you gets you all flustered."

"I guess so," I said with a blush.

Caleb gave me another long, slow kiss.

I could feel him hard against my back, so I changed my position a bit so I could take him inside me.

"Ohh, baby, you're sore. You don't have to..." Caleb groaned.

"I want to." I moved delicately up and down his shaft, leaning back against him and curling one arm behind his neck.

This, of course, made my breasts stick out, and Caleb couldn't resist. While I rode him slowly, he grasped my breasts and played with them. "So perfect..." he murmured.

I closed my eyes at the tingling sensations his attention sent through me. It even made riding him easier. I was sore, but it also felt oh-so-good.

Caleb kissed my shoulder, then nuzzled my ear. "You gonna come on my cock?"

I shivered. "Yes, Caleb. I am going to come on your cock."

"I'm going to cum inside, which means I'll just have to wash my dirty girl again," Caleb teased.

I turned my head so I could kiss him on the lips. "I'm your dirty girl."

"Fuck yes." Caleb began thrusting upward as I ground down on him.

He erupted inside me as pleasure shot through my body. Caleb kissed me and squeezed my breasts and bounced me on his lap until we were both spent.

Then, true to his word, he slipped me off his dick and started washing me there again.

I let him, this time just relaxing against him and enjoying his touch.

We were just slowly getting out of the large tub, touching and kissing, when there was a knock at the door.

"Coming!" Caleb called, frowning slightly at the interruption. We found a couple of large, soft white robes in the bathroom and put them on.

Caleb opened the door to see a grim-looking older version of Will. "Mr. Masterson Senior, sir," Caleb said respectfully.

I felt almost as though I should curtsy. That was the kind of presence Mr. Masterson had.

"Caleb." Mr. Masterson acknowledged him with an incline of his head. "And you must be Jacey."

"Yes, sir," I swallowed. "Have we outstayed our welcome?"

Mr. Masterson's expression softened. "No, dear. I'm sorry, I tend to be intimidating, they say. Good for the boardroom. Bad for meeting new people." His smile faded. "But I do have a Mr. Collins outside looking for you."

"Don't let him in," Caleb said quickly. "He's trying to intimidate Jacey into dropping the charges against him."

Mr. Masterson nodded. "Martha," he called. "Have security escort Mr. Collins off of our property."

"How did he even find out where I was?" I asked, feeling the color drain from my cheeks.

"Hmm. That is an excellent question. One I might have a private detective look into," Mr. Masterson murmured. "Though... you're pressing charges against your father? For... oh my, I suppose for that very nasty bruise on your cheek."

I touched my cheek. I'd almost forgotten. "Yes. It was a cut, but they stitched it up at Urgent Care."

"I'll have one of my attorneys file a restraining order against him," Mr. Masterson said. "I'm glad you're here, though it is a rather odd circumstance. Caleb being your stepbrother and all."

Caleb groaned and I blushed. "It just... sort of happened," I explained.

"Oh, you don't owe me any explanations. I'd just been talking over why we had new guests with Will. He neglected to tell me, you see," Mr. Masterson sighed. "That boy..."

"I'm sure he'll be a much better doctor than he is a communicator," Caleb grinned.

"I hope so. Why don't you two come out for some fresh air? Martha can turn over your linens, then," Mr. Masterson suggested.

I gasped and ran toward the bed, stripping it like a madwoman. "I am not going to make her touch this! Is there a place where I can do the laundry?"

Mr. Masterson chuckled. "It was nice of you to strip the bed, but let Martha handle it. She's rather possessive over the washing machines."

"Oh." I set the sheets and comforter down.

"All right then. You two come out and we'll all have some lunch," Mr. Masterson said. "I don't have to be back in Singapore for two days."

"We'll be right out, sir," Caleb replied.

Mr. Masterson left us to it.

Caleb and I quickly got dressed-in clothes that were exactly our size that Martha had hung in the closet.

"This is better than a hotel," I remarked.

"Absolutely," Caleb said. He buttoned up a blue shirt that was just a few shades darker than his eyes. "How do I look?"

"Like Dr. Caleb Killeen," I smiled.

"Good." Caleb then sat on the edge of the mattress and watched me dress in a soft, yellow sundress. "That looks good on you."

"Thanks." I went to the bathroom to fluff my hair a bit then took Caleb's hand and walked out into the sunlight.

It stung a bit after being under artificial light for so long, but my eyes soon adjusted. Caleb led me out to a nice outdoor veranda where a white, wrought iron table was sitting, surrounded by chairs. It had a sun umbrella over it.

Will was already there, as was Mr. Masterson I waved at them.

"Welcome, my dear," Mr. Masterson said. "Caleb, do pull out a chair for the young lady."

Caleb chuckled. I could tell he'd already been primed to do that.

I sat to Mr. Masterson's left, Will at his right, and Caleb next to me.

"So." Mr. Masterson put down his lemonade. "Tell me about Canada."

"Canada?" I squeaked, surprised.

"You... know," Caleb replied shrewdly.

Mr. Masterson nodded. "A rather unscrupulous business associate of mine runs several illegal logging operations up that way. He was complaining over brandy and cigars about two kids almost ruining the whole endeavor. A man named Girard Barbier managed to 'handle the situation.' My business associate dropped your name, Caleb. Imagine my surprise."

"You can tell your business associate we have no intention of testifying. I'm calling a truce. Too many people keep dying," Caleb said.

"Ah. So no Canadian witness protection for you," Mr. Masterson inferred.

"No." Caleb took my hand under the table. "No, the cost is just too high."

"Caleb. You are only responsible for one of those deaths, and that was self-defense. Please don't continue to beat yourself up," Mr. Masterson responded kindly.

Caleb rubbed the back of his neck with his free hand. "It's hard not to, sir."

"I know. You two were just starting some proper therapy, yes? Well, considering Mr. Collins was trying to storm the castle, I will get two private therapists to come here," Mr. Masterson said. "As for my business associate, I will make sure to keep a close eye on the situation."

"Thank you, sir," I replied softly.

Martha then brought out some sandwiches and more lemonade.

Will dug right in, eyeing Caleb in a way that told me he had a ton of questions to spring on him once his father was gone.

I ate more slowly. My father had probably come to plead his case. Maybe I should have heard him out?

"Forget Hank," Caleb murmured to me. "Forget him. He made his bed."

"Agreed," Mr. Masterson said. He patted my shoulder. "You're doing the right thing."

I sighed and nodded. I really hoped I was doing the right thing.

16

FIGHTING THE GOOD FIGHT

-Caleb-

"Baby, I'm here. I'm right here," I told Jacey as we entered the district attorney's office.

It had been a few days, and I'd slept blissfully well, but Jacey had tossed and turned, still unsure about accusing her father of assault.

When the district attorney called us, Jacey was already a wreck. So there was no way I was letting her go alone.

We were shown to a small office where a young attorney was sitting.

"Jacey. Caleb," the attorney said. "My name is Nathan Kirby. I'm handling the case against your father. Please, sit."

Jacey and I sat down.

"Now, the way I see it, things are pretty cut and dried. We have the evidence of the assault that we need. I don't even see this going to trial. Your father would be smart to take a plea," Nathan went on.

"What sort of plea?" I asked.

"We're offering community service. It's his first offense," Nathan explained.

I frowned. "Community... service...?"

"I know it doesn't seem like a lot," Nathan said.

"It seems like a slap on the wrist," I argued.

"He still gets an assault charge on his record. And I have the restraining order here for you to sign." Nathan pulled out some papers.

I looked at Jacey, who was now pale and staring at the papers, wringing her hands in her lap.

"Will social services keep an eye on the situation once the baby is born?" I asked.

"For a while. If they don't find any reason to keep following up, they'll stop," Nathan answered with a wince.

I supposed my expression was just as thunderous as I felt. "This is bullshit."

"Does it even matter if I press charges, then?" Jacey whispered.

"It will matter more if he repeats his offense." Nathan spread his hands helplessly. "There is only so much the law can do."

I shook my head. "This is such bullshit."

"I want to drop the charges," Jacey said.

My eyes widened, and I looked at Jacey. She wouldn't look at me.

Nathan smiled. "It is nice when families can just work things out together."

"But I'm signing the restraining order," Jacey corrected him.

"Oh. Well, here it is." Nathan slid the papers across the desk.

I put my hand over Jacey's pale ones. "Jacey, is this what you really want?"

Jacey nodded. "Yes."

"Baby, look at me." Jacey finally glanced up, her eyes shimmering with tears.

"Are you disappointed?" she asked softly.

"Oh, baby, no. No. You should do what you think is right. I'll support any decision you make," I replied, squeezing her clenched hands.

Jacey gave me a watery smile then brought one hand up to sign the restraining order.

"There. That's done. I'll make sure this gets filed with the court," Nathan said. He smiled at us. "Thank you for coming in."

I had a feeling the asshole had wanted us to come in just so that Jacey would drop the case, and he'd have one less thing he had to deal with. But I didn't say anything. I stood with Jacey and took her hand in mine and stalked out of the attorney's office.

"You *are* mad," Jacey murmured as I walked double-time to get out of the building.

"Hmm? Oh, baby, not at you. At that dickhead we just met with. I can't believe how stupid the whole thing is. Law my ass," I grumbled.

"It was a bit... disappointing," Jacey admitted.

I put an arm around her and tucked her into my side as we walked. "I'm sorry, baby."

"Not your fault." Jacey kissed my jawline. "At least now we can go back to Will's and forget all of this."

"Good point," I said. "I'll–" I stopped, feeling as though we were being watched. I turned, then pushed Jacey protectively behind me.

"Caleb, I want to talk with my daughter," Hank demanded, standing with my mother outside a car that had just come up and parked behind us.

"You're going to get towed. Better head off," I said icily.

Hank ignored me. "Jacey, please. Drop the charges..."

"She did. Now scram," I interrupted.

Jacey put a calming hand on my back and peeked her head around my arm. "Dad, I've filed a restraining order against you. You can't be this close to me."

Hank looked pained. "Restraining order? But you're my daughter..."

"Should have thought of that before you split open her cheek," I snapped.

"That never should have happened. I'm sorry. I got completely the wrong idea, I..." Hank started to approach us.

I moved backward, making Jacey step back as well.

"We got a problem here?" Will asked, popping up next to me.

"Yeah," I said. "That's Hank."

"The wife-beater?" Will asked.

Hank puffed out his chest. "I would never beat my wife!"

"Oh, yeah, just your daughter. Sorry, I got confused," Will snorted.

Hank deflated. "I'm sorry. I am. Please, both of you, come home."

"No," Jacey replied softly behind me.

"What?" Hank asked.

"She said 'no,' now step off!" I shouted.

Hank's face fell. "I just... I want us to be a family."

"I can't, Dad. I can't right now. I can hardly look at you," Jacey said. "Please... just... leave us alone."

My mother walked up to Hank and put a hand on his shoulder. "Let's go home, love. They're just not ready today."

"Okay." Hank trudged back toward his car. "I'll... I'll try again later." He got in and so did my mother.

Will waved at them sarcastically as they drove away. "All right, let's blow this popsicle stand."

Jacey smiled, and I breathed out a sigh of relief. "Yeah. Let's."

WILL'S pool was more like a grotto with a hidden cave behind a small waterfall feature that had nice mood lighting.

I privately had a word with Will, and he let us have the pool all to ourselves. But still, I wasn't going to fuck Jacey in open daylight.

So I coaxed her into the snug little haven.

"Caleb, why do you want to go in there when we have the whole pool to swim in?" Jacey asked me, wrinkling her nose as the waterfall feature doused her beautiful black hair.

It also doused her bikini top, making her nipples stand out prettily against the wet fabric. "Mhm," I said absently.

"Caleb!" Jacey swatted me. "What are we doing back here?"

"This." I fused my lips to hers.

Jacey squeaked then clung to my shoulders as I licked her lips and found entry to her mouth.

When we came up for air, Jacey gasped, "Caleb, we can't! What if someone sees?"

"No one can see in here. And I told Will to keep the pool off limits," I replied.

Jacey blushed in the low light. "You want to do it in here?"

"There, now we're on the same page." I kissed her again.

Jacey hesitated then her hand descended into the waistband of my swim shorts to grip my cock.

"That's my girl," I murmured, hard and ready before she even started stroking. I pulled the strings of her bikini top, and it fell away, revealing creamy skin and peaked rose nipples.

"Oh, baby, what you do to me," I murmured. I moved the thin strip of her bikini bottoms aside to push two fingers into her ready entrance.

"What do I do to you?" Jacey whispered, grinding down on my hand.

"Fuck, baby, you make me weak at the knees." I moaned as Jacey and I took care of each other. I finished in my shorts while Jacey cried out and came around my fingers.

I pulled Jacey into my lap, shoving my shorts down and holding her bikini bottoms aside so I could spear her on my dick. Jacey gasped and put her arms around my neck. She started to ride me without prompting.

"Baby, you're so good to me. Yeah, just like that. Juuust like that." I buried my face in her beautiful breasts while I helped her ease up and down on me with my hands on her hips.

Jacey pulled my head up for a kiss, and I devoured her mouth like I devoured her body. I was ravenous.

"You're so *big* today," Jacey panted, throwing her head back as I started bringing her body down for deep, sharp thrusts.

Yeah, my baby was tight around my dick. I didn't know if I was bigger or she was just a little tighter today. Maybe from stress? At any rate, neither of us were complaining as Jacey bounced up and down on my cock, and her breasts slapped me in the face.

"Come for me, baby. Show me you like my big dick," I murmured, keeping up the punishing pace.

With a sob of pleasure, Jacey clung to me and came, milking my dick vigorously.

"Yeah... baby... yeah... take it all..." I groaned, holding her hips flush to mine so I was buried as deep as I could go.

Jacey took it, every drop. She held onto me until the very last twitch of my dick. Then she sagged against my chest.

"Oh, no, baby. We're not done yet," I said, stroking her wet hair. "Fuck me, you're so tight I could cum again without moving a muscle."

Jacey gave me a tired smile. "But you don't like to cum without me."

"True." I fondled her breast. "I start a new job tomorrow. And then I'll be able to apply for an apartment."

"A studio," Jacey said.

"I can afford a one-bedro-" I began.

Jacey shook her head emphatically. "A studio. I want us both to save as much money as we can." Then she blinked. "Oh. I need a job, too!"

I wanted to argue with her, but I couldn't. She was right. It would be best if we both had jobs.

"We also need to start looking at scholarships," I said. "Damn, this is not going to be the smoothest of adventures, baby."

Jacey stroked my chest, skimming a palm over my nipple. "We've had adventures that haven't gone so well before. At least this one won't involve a gun."

"I hope not. I still don't know if Mom's told your dad about us," I pointed out.

"He saw me kiss you on the street..." Jacey said.

"He saw you basically kiss my cheek," I responded. "That's not exactly... proof positive of a relationship other than brother and sister."

Jacey gave me a wicked smile. "Would you ever do this with your sister?" She swiveled her hips.

I groaned. "No. So thank God we're not related." I kissed her, squeezing the breast I'd been fondling.

She giggled against my lips. "I'm glad it was you, Caleb. I always wanted it to be you."

"It's always going to be me. No other man is ever, *ever*, going to fuck you ever. Ever," I said possessively.

"Oh, are you going to fuck me?" Jacey teased.

I growled and pressed her up against the cave wall. "Until you can't remember your own name."

"Good," Jacey grinned and kissed me again.

17

SECRETS AND LIES

-Jacey-

I woke in the early hours, when it was still dark. At first, I didn't know what had woken me, but then Caleb thrashed his head back and forth and groaned.

"Caleb," I whispered, cupping his cheek. "Caleb, it's a bad dream..."

Caleb swatted at my hand, his eyelids flying open. At first, he stared into the near-darkness lit only by a digital clock, unseeing. Then he saw me and sighed heavily, wrapping me in his arms. "I'm sorry," he murmured. "Did I hurt you?"

"No." I touched him carefully, slowly bringing him into reality. "Caleb, I love you. I hate that you keep having these nightmares." I spread my hand over his heart.

"Me, too." Caleb nuzzled the top of my head. "Oh God, me, too."

"We need to go to therapists," I said softly. "We keep putting it off..."

Caleb laughed bitterly. "Pretty sure we don't have health insurance."

"Oh." I frowned at this realization. "That's... not good..."

"No." Caleb feathered kisses over my forehead.

He wanted me. He was already leaking against my leg.

Still, I tried to get reason to prevail. "This isn't always going to be the answer, Caleb."

"It works for us. For now." Caleb snuggled me and gave me a kiss, his hands starting to wander.

Caleb rolled me underneath him.

"Maybe we should try talking...?" I suggested.

Caleb shook his head slowly. When I felt the head of him at my entrance, I gave up and gave in, wrapping my arms around him as he sank his cock deep inside me.

"That's my girl," Caleb whispered, kissing me as he started out at a leisurely pace. The push and pull of him inside me was almost agonizingly slow.

I whimpered and bucked my hips.

"Patience, baby. I'm gonna give it to you good," Caleb said. He kept his slow and steady pace, rolling my nipples between his fingertips.

"You always give it to me good," I breathed, trying to get more friction.

But Caleb would not be hurried. "You said you wanted to talk."

"While you're fucking me?!" I protested.

Caleb grinned. "Well, when am I not?"

He had a point. I tried to get my brain to concentrate. "I... nightmares... bad..."

"Mhm. Very bad." Caleb didn't speed up one bit.

"T-Talk to me about them..." My teeth chattered.

"Needy baby," Caleb teased. "Wants my cock. Wants my dreams..."

"You're the one who... who said I could have both!" I reminded him.

Caleb sobered and nodded. "It's probably easier this way."

"G-Good," I said.

With a long, slow kiss, Caleb began. "I keep seeing the Mounties.

And Bill... and the detective. Just... the blood and other... stuff. It gets worse every night. Their eyes..." Caleb shuddered and I felt it in my core.

I stroked his cheek. "Baby, that's awful. I wish I could take that for you."

"I'd rather it be me if it has to be one of us," Caleb murmured.

"I know. And I wish the opposite. Guess there's no way we'll come to an agreement about that." I twirled the longish hair on top of his head between my fingers.

"Is this our first fight?" Caleb chuckled.

I bucked my hips again. "It will be if you don't fuck me properly, Caleb Killeen."

"Mmm. I like this side of you. All bossy." Caleb grinned at me and started thrusting in earnest.

"Please... Caleb... harder..." I begged.

Caleb raised his eyebrows. "Baby, you usually don't-"

I gripped his face in my hands. "Make me come."

"Yes, ma'am." Caleb did something positively sinful with his hips before riding me hard. He ground his thumb against my clit.

I cried out in pleasure, clamping my legs around Caleb's waist as I arched into him.

"Ohh... yeah, baby." Caleb's warm cum filled me up.

I stroked my hands over his strong muscles as he finished, trembling, in my arms. "I love you, Caleb. I want you to be happy."

"You make me happy." Caleb kissed me soundly. "I love you. You make me happy."

"Even when you're not... dick deep in me?" I asked with a self-conscious wince.

Caleb laughed at that. "Baby, you're my joy. Sure, I like being dick-deep in you. I like it a lot. But I also like that you can't bluff for shit when we play cards. And that you hum when you wash your hair. And you hold me when I have bad dreams." Caleb kissed me again. "You're very generous with your body, baby, but you're so much more generous with your heart."

I beamed at him. "I'm glad."

"So?" Caleb asked.

"So... what?" I responded.

"So... do I make you happy, even when I'm not dick-deep in you?" Caleb smiled.

I cuddled him. "I get excited every time I see you and sad when we're apart. I don't know if that will last forever, but I do know you're always going to be my heart and soul. You don't need to be dick deep in me. I mean, I really like it, too..." I blushed. "So it's not really any great sacrifice to spread my legs for you, but... that's not why I love you."

"Spread your legs for me," Caleb chuckled. "Makes me sound like I've come to pillage your town."

"I feel pillaged. You've got a really big pillager." I clenched my inner muscles around the pillager in question.

Caleb grinned. "You say the nicest things."

Then, he had me again.

***

CALEB and I hunched over one of Will's tablets, searching for work in the Twin Cities area. Preferably something that wouldn't be far from campus for me.

Will drank a cocktail and watched us with a smile on his face. "You two are just cuter than a puddle of puppies."

I snorted, but Caleb drew a sharp breath.

"Where did you hear that?" Caleb asked flatly.

Will sat up. "Woah, mood change."

"I asked you where you heard that phrase," Caleb demanded.

Caleb was tense, more tense than even when he woke up from one of his nightmares. I put a hand on his arm. "Caleb?"

"My dad says it, why?" Will replied with a frown.

Caleb trembled under my hand. "Girard said the same thing."

My hands flew to my mouth. "Oh God... no..."

"That's weird. It's not a really common phrase," Will said slowly.

"No," Caleb grunted. "It's not."

"Caleb?" I whispered.

Caleb set the tablet down and folded his hands, regarding Will. "Who's the 'business associate' of your father who runs the illegal logging operation?"

"I... I don't know, man, I didn't ask," Will said defensively.

Caleb stood, the wrought iron patio chair scraping backward. "Where's your father's office?"

"No way, dude. You can't go in there," Will responded, shaking his head emphatically. "The last time I went in there... shit, man. I don't even want to remember it."

"Well, guess what? I'm going in," Caleb said. "So you can either help me find it or stay out of my way." Caleb stalked toward the house. I scurried to follow him.

Will got up and tried to head him off. "Really, Caleb, you can't go ransacking the house–"

"I can and I will," Caleb growled. He started opening doors.

"Caleb, stop! If you think my dad did something wrong, I'll look into it. But don't tear the house ap-no, not in there!" Will gasped, grabbing for the doorknob.

Caleb was faster. The door pushed open into a kind of security office, only there was no guard, just monitors showing different images of the property.

It took me a beat before I realized, besides outside security, the only camera views were in Caleb's and my bedroom. And bathroom. And the veranda where we spent most of our time.

"Oh my God..." I gasped.

There was even a camera in the pool cave.

Caleb stared for a long time and then rounded on Will. "You've been spying on us?"

"It's not what you think. I wasn't making a porno or anything. My dad just said I needed to keep an eye on you–" Will made a little 'eep' when Caleb grabbed him by the throat.

"You *watched* Jacey and me?!" Caleb snarled.

"Well," Will said in a strangled tone. "In your defense, you two really could be porn stars. I mean what you do is HOT."

It was the wrong thing to say. I knew it. And about five seconds later, Will knew it, too.

Caleb punched Will in the face. Repeatedly.

I grabbed Caleb's arm. "No, Caleb! Stop!"

Caleb's fist hovered in the air. Then he dropped Will to the floor. Will coughed and bled.

"It's your father who runs the illegal mining operation in Canada, isn't it?" Caleb asked. "*Isn't* it?!"

"Look, you're my friend. But he's my dad. He pays for my life. All you two had to do -- have to do – is hang around here. He'll even pay for your tuition, I'll bet. He just doesn't want you to go reporting to the authorities again," Will choked out.

"For your information, we weren't going to," Caleb seethed. "But now... now..."

I felt sick looking at the screens. "Did you... record us?"

Caleb's eyes lit with new fury. "Yeah, did you record us?"

Will shook his head emphatically. "No. Me and Charlie just watched, that's all. No recordings. All live feed."

"Who the FUCK is Charlie?!" Caleb asked.

"The day guard. Look, as long as you're with me, he can do his rounds or go on break or whatever. This isn't a bad deal, Caleb. I promise,' Will said.

Caleb loomed over him. "You and I have a very different idea of what a 'bad deal' is."

"I'm sure the old man will pay for both your colleges. I mean, all the way up through med school and residency and everything, Caleb," Will pleaded. "All you have to do is prove to him that you're loyal."

"Like I told your dad – I don't want any part in the whole logging business. I just want out. Jacey, too. But this, Will, this is crossing one hell of a line," Caleb growled.

"What are you going to do?" Will asked, gathering himself up and holding his broken nose. "Where are you going to go?"

Caleb scowled at Will. "I don't know. But I do know it's none of your damn business." Caleb put a protective arm around me, and we headed for the front door.

"Girard was right. You are a troublesome twosome," Mr. Masterson said, suddenly appearing around the corner.

"Fuck." Caleb kept motoring me toward the door until there was a telltale click.

I squeezed my eyes shut. "It's another gun, isn't it?"

"It's another gun," Caleb confirmed.

"We're being kidnapped again, aren't we?" I asked.

"You're being kidnapped again," Mr. Masterson said.

I swallowed as Caleb turned us to face Mr. Masterson. "Where are we going?" I inquired.

"You have a few options. How did you enjoy being a lumberjack, Caleb?" Mr. Masterson asked sweetly.

Caleb's answer was a dark grunt.

"No to that, then. I have a villa in Montenegro?" Mr. Masterson suggested.

"Pass," Caleb said flatly.

"Really? Most people would kill for a worry-free life in Montenegro," Mr. Masterson said.

Caleb's eyes narrowed. "I have killed. And it's not worth the blood money."

"Blood moncy. No one was getting hurt until you came along, Caleb," Mr. Masterson tsked.

I scowled at Mr. Masterson. "Are you suggesting all this was Caleb's fault?"

"Well, I'm not suggesting he should have let that Bill fellow rape you, but you both have made all the wrong moves since then," Mr. Masterson accused.

"What's door number three?" I asked before Caleb's white hot anger could get out of control.

"You go home," Mr. Masterson said simply. "To your father and stepmother. I have business dealings–legitimate business dealings– with your father. He'll see the light."

I shook my head. "I don't want this spilling over onto the baby."

"My dear, it is far too late for that," Mr. Masterson chuckled.

"Home," Caleb said.

I looked up at him. "What?"

"We're going home. We'll go home, for now. Jacey starts college in the fall, and I will be working. I plan on getting an apartment for us," Caleb continued. "But for now, we'll go home. Is that agreeable?"

"We'll renegotiate in a few months. I'll let it slide, I think... if you come work for me, Caleb," Mr. Masterson replied.

Caleb stared at him. "Work... for you?"

"Yes. Not as a lumberjack, but in the corporate office. You have a good head on your shoulders, and I need a new personal assistant." Mr. Masterson's smile became wide and evil. "And in that capacity, your hands will get as dirty as mine."

"Caleb..." Maybe Montenegro wasn't such a bad idea?

Caleb kissed the top of my head. "I accept."

Mr. Masterson clapped his hands. "Excellent! You start on Monday. Take the rest of the week and the weekend to get settled back at home."

Caleb nodded and turned back to the door, walking stiffly toward it. We both knew there was still a gun at our back, and one wrong move could result in catastrophe.

"Oh, Caleb?" Mr. Masterson called.

Caleb turned his head slightly. "Yes?"

"Do drop by and visit from time to time. You and Jacey are such lovely people. We'd love to have you for dinner," Mr. Masterson said.

Caleb didn't answer. He and I just walked faster out the door.

18

———————————————

DEAL WITH THE DEVIL

-Caleb-

"I knew you'd be back," Hank said triumphantly when we showed up at the door.

"I'm sure you did," I replied icily.

"Mr. Masterson. He's good people. Knows when to send kids home." Hank was all puffed up and strutting around as though he had won a victory.

It was infuriating.

We should have gone to Montenegro.

"Guess we'd just better get back to our rooms," I said through my teeth. I glared at my mother. "Same house rules?"

My mother wrung her hands and looked at Hank.

"What house rules?" Hank asked.

Ah. That answered that question. Hank still didn't know.

"I... suppose I may have been too harsh before," my mother replied softly.

"Harsh? That boy needs to respect you–" Hank began.

My mother held up her hand. "It was me who disrespected him. And Jacey."

Hank blinked. "Oh."

"Yeah. Oh," I grunted.

"Well." Hank puffed up again. "You can get to your rooms, then. Probably have some cleaning or organizing or who knows what to do."

"Definitely have something to do." *Your daughter.*

Jacey sighed and headed for the bedrooms.

"'Welcome home, Caleb and Jacey. We missed you,'" I grumbled under my breath as I followed Jacey. I still showed some semblance of propriety by going in my bedroom door and not hers, but once we got settled and I did a walk-through of my room, I went straight through the bathroom and into Jacey's room.

Jacey was rearranging the Care Bears on her bed. I came up behind her and wrapped my arms around her, kissing her neck. "Everything still where you left it?"

"No. Jeanie must have cleaned. And snooped. My diary's gone," Jacey mumbled, pointing to her bedside dresser.

"Yeah, I saw that in my room, too. That Mom cleaned." I frowned and released Jacey to go back into my room. "Well fuck."

"What?" Jacey asked.

"She took our condoms, lube... uh... magazines I used to have..." I coughed.

Jacey giggled. "Now, Caleb, were you a naughty boy with dirty magazines?"

"I was. Naughty, naughty me," I grinned.

Jacey walked through the bathroom into my room and snuggled up to me. I wrapped my arms around her.

"I'll bet you want to be a naughty boy with me," she whispered, brushing her lips over mine.

Good. We both needed Hank-is-being-an-asshat sex. Or maybe it was Mr.-Masterson-is-an-asshat sex.

I grabbed her ass and ground against her, letting her feel how hard I was. "Get naked and get on all fours," I murmured hotly in her ear.

Jacey did as she was told, stripping and getting into position on my bed. She looked back at me over her shoulder, her dark hair cascading down to my sheets.

I didn't bother with clothes. I could see her core was dripping wet for me. So I didn't bother with foreplay, either. I simply unzipped, got behind her, and plunged my cock inside.

Her walls stretched around me, and Jacey mewled, arching her back like a cat.

I pulled back and thrust again, slapping her ass as I did so.

Jacey jumped, her insides tightening reflexively around me.

"Oh, baby, do that again," I groaned. I pulled back and spanked her again, thrusting deep as I did so.

Jacey whimpered. At first, I thought she was going to object to the spanking, but then she said, "It's too much, Caleb. I'm going to come."

"My pretty baby. Are you going to come on my cock?" I asked, rubbing the red spot where I'd spanked her.

Jacey did come then, squeezing around my dick, her arms giving, and she dropped forward onto her elbows.

I wrapped her hair around my fist and pulled just hard enough for it to sting a little bit, then started riding her hard.

She came twice more, shuddering and fisting around my cock, then begged for mercy.

I thrust a few more times, then released into her with a groan, making sure she took every drop of my cum.

Jacey made a sound in her throat when I pulled out.

"Don't worry, baby," I said, rolling her onto her back. "It's going back in."

To emphasize my words, I pushed every inch of my thick dick back into her.

She gasped and gripped my wrists as I hovered over her. "How can you possibly want more?!"

I nuzzled her and gave her a soft kiss. "I always want more."

"I'm sore," Jacey complained.

"I'll be gentle," I said. "Please?"

Jacey sighed and widened her legs.

I wrapped them around my waist, then just rocked in her, my thrusts slow and shallow.

Jacey closed her eyes and let her body enjoy mine. I knew I was enjoying hers.

Finally, she orgasmed with a gasp, and I came, filling her up again.

We laid together in a tangle of arms and legs for what felt like hours, blissfully drifting in and out of sleep.

"Are you worried?" Jacey asked.

"About what?" I replied.

"Working for Mr. Masterson." Jacey looked up at me with wide, concerned eyes.

I sighed. "Yes. I'm worried. I'm more worried I'm going to find out about human trafficking or something really bad than I am about the actual work itself."

"Human trafficking would be bad," Jacey agreed.

"But it's what I have to do to keep us safe." I kissed the top of her head. "Don't worry too much. As long as we're together, things are never as bad as they seem."

Jacey put a hand over my heart. "I love you. I don't want you to have to do this."

"No choice," I replied. I took her hand and kissed it. "I love you, too. We'll figure this out. Don't worry."

"Okay," Jacey said.

There was a knock on my door. "Dinner," my mother called.

"Thank you!" I called back. "Let's go eat. We can talk more later."

Jacey nodded, and we got up and got dressed to go eat.

Hopefully Hank was done being insufferable for the day.

AS I ADJUSTED my blue tie for the third time, I decided to focus on the positive. Namely that I was getting out of the house. Hank had been gloating over our return nonstop from the time we arrived to this very morning at breakfast. Only Jacey's calming presence had stopped me from throttling him.

I walked across the busy downtown Minneapolis street toward MacMillan Masterson Incorporated's corporate headquarters feeling as though I were trudging toward the gallows. I was about to be inducted into a criminal enterprise. This was not exactly a dream future for a doctor-hopeful.

Before I could enter the building, though, a man in a black suit grabbed my arm. "Please come with me," he said in a no-nonsense tone.

"Are you the welcoming committee?" I asked dryly, following him to a coffee shop that was just back the way I had come.

The man was silent. I began to get a little weirded out when he knew my coffee order, though.

He gestured for me to sit at a table in the corner. "We don't have much time," he said. He reached into his pocket, glanced around to see if anyone was watching, then flashed his badge. "I'm agent Darren Church of the FBI. We've had William MacMillan Masterson Sr. under surveillance for some time now. We know he's a criminal." He gave me a hard stare. "And you know he's a criminal."

Oh fuck. I stood quickly. "Hey man. I don't know what you're running, but I'm out. I've had all I'm going to take of law enforcement in this lifetime."

"Caleb," Darren replied. "Think carefully about this. He's going down one way or another. You don't want to go down with him. Just go in there and get some information. That's all I'm asking. Keep us abreast of what's going on. Is that so hard?"

"I'm not getting my girlfriend and me killed," I snapped back. "Take whatever you're offering and shove it." I started to leave.

Darren grabbed my arm again. "Here," he said, tucking his card into my jacket pocket. "Just in case you change your mind."

"I won't." I hurried out of the coffee shop and back over to the MacMillan Masterson building.

"Took you long enough," a grumpy woman in a pencil skirt with a tight bun said once I checked in with the guard. "I was starting to think you weren't coming."

"Sorry. I got a bit sidetracked," I responded.

The woman snapped a picture of me. "You'll have your official badge by the end of the day. For now... Rodrigo, please give Mr. Killeen a visitor's badge."

Rodrigo handed over a badge on a blue lanyard, then the woman motioned for me to follow her. She didn't waste any time, either. I had no idea how she moved so fast in such a tight skirt and high heels.

"My name is Jessica Price. You may call me Jessica. I'm the head of human resources. Since you're going to be Mr. Masterson's new assistant, I wanted to handle your onboarding personally," Jessica said.

I nodded my understanding. "Thank you so much for taking the time, Jessica."

"You're welcome." Jessica's tone didn't make it sound as though I was welcome, however. She pressed her badge to an elevator key reader, then pressed it again when we got inside. "You're on the hundred-and-fiftieth floor. Your badge will get you there tomorrow, but a visitor's badge doesn't have that kind of clearance. So I'd suggest not going out to lunch today unless you're with Mr. Masterson."

"Or one of the other staff?" I assumed.

Jessica shook her head. "None of the staff are allowed to card anyone else in. Even if it's known staff. It's a fireable infraction."

"Good to know," I said.

Jessica click-clicked across the slate flooring once the elevator doors opened on the 150th floor. There was a cheerful receptionist at a large desk sitting in front of a wall with a huge sign reading "MacMillan Masterson Incorporated" over her head. The words stood out from the wall and were a silver color in a professional script.

"Lacy, this is Caleb, Mr. Masterson's new assistant. Caleb, this is Lacy. She handles everything you don't," Jessica informed me.

"Hi!" Lacy beamed. "I heard you were starting today. It's so nice to meet you!"

I managed a smile. "Nice to meet you, too."

"All right, off we go to see your work area. Mr. Masterson is in today, so I'm sure he'll want to talk to you as well," Jessica said in a bored tone.

"Of course," I replied, trying not to sound too disappointed. I'd rather hoped he'd be back in Singapore.

Jessica showed me to a glass-topped desk sitting right outside large wooden double doors. I decided this must be the entrance to Mr. Masterson's office. "This is your station. Should you ever need to leave it for any reason –bathroom break, whatever – you need to let Lacy know so she can field Mr. Masterson's calls. Now, we're going to log on to your computer and start getting you set up on the systems. There should be several e-mails in your inbox with IDs and temporary passwords–"

The door to Mr. Masterson's office opened, and the man himself walked out. "Caleb! I was so afraid you weren't going to make it today. Jessica, would you mind excusing us for a minute? I'll call you when we're finished, and then you can finish getting Caleb settled in."

"Yes, of course, sir," Jessica said, finally smiling professionally.

So she wasn't a grump to everyone.

"This way, Caleb." Mr. Masterson put an arm around me and ushered me into his office.

"Sir," I managed to utter respectfully. "Forgive me if I say I'm not really interested in going to lunch with you."

"I understand completely. Hopefully we can change that attitude of yours over time," Mr. Masterson chuckled. "I just wanted to tell you I was talking to Hank."

This couldn't be good.

"He and I have decided I should take Jacey on as an intern. She'll be Lacy's assistant. Lacy could use the help. Especially since you're just getting trained," Mr. Masterson said.

I was right. It was terrible news. "I thought we were keeping Jacey out of this," I growled.

"Did you? No. I think not. You're both in it neck deep." Mr. Masterson's voice was now flat and unyielding. "I'm not going to let either of you go to Darren Church. Did you have a nice coffee this morning?"

I felt the blood drain from my face. "I didn't know who he was."

"I know. He grabs all of the newbies and tries to scare them into ratting me out. Unfortunately, the pay's too good." Mr. Masterson smiled at me. "You are going to be paid very handsomely, Caleb. More than if you'd become a doctor."

My jaw clenched. "It was never about the money."

"I know. But I wanted to let you know there are at least some positives of working this job. Now, I'm going to call Jessica back and have her get you up to speed. I'm sure you'll be working closely with Lacy as well. And Jacey." Mr. Masterson was quite pleased with himself, I could tell.

"If you don't mind, I'll just go wait for Jessica to come back," I seethed.

Mr. Masterson waved a hand. "Go ahead. Oh, and Caleb?"

"Yes?" I asked.

"See you at lunch," he said.

19

THE INTERN

-Jacey-

"I don't like it."

I glanced up at Caleb's thunderous expression as I finished adjusting his tie. "I know, love. I know. But it's not like we have a choice. Dad's ecstatic."

"Of course he is." Caleb blew out a long breath, then thumbed the collar of my red blazer. "I don't want you pulled into this mess. I —"

I leaned up and kissed him, then wiped some of my understated red lipstick off his lips. "You've said. I'll be okay. Besides, you'll be there."

"I know." Caleb hugged me hard.

"Caleb, you're going to wrinkle both of us," I scolded him. But I wasn't really mad. I was terrified and happy for the hug.

Caleb didn't let go right away. "I love you so much. If anything were to happen to you..."

"You'd go scorched earth. I know. I feel the same way," I replied.

Caleb finally released me. We both patted and smoothed each other down, then looked in my mirror again.

"Mr. Killeen, you look quite dashing today," I said, trying to lighten the mood.

Caleb gave me a small smile. "And you, Miss Collins, look quite fetching."

I put my hand in his and let Caleb lead me out to his Prius.

"Have fun, you two!" Jeanie called.

I almost cringed. Yeah. Fun.

My father was already at work, but we'd received similar well-wishes the night before. "Just think how good it will look on your resume!" he'd crowed at dinner.

I'd rather burn my resume and live in a box for the rest of my life than work for Mr. Masterson. But I also liked Caleb and me to be alive and breathing. Hence: Internship.

Caleb buckled me in, his aftershave wafting over me, then went around the other side of the car and buckled up himself. Then, whether we liked it or not, we were off.

When we got to MacMillan Masterson, Caleb glanced around, a suspicious look on his face. He seemed to spot someone, and a scowl came over his features. He put a strong arm around me, looking off at that someone I couldn't identify in the crowd, and escorted me hurriedly into the building.

"That's Jessica," he whispered when we reached the front desk. "She's the head of HR. She's not exactly friendly, but she is knowl-edgeable."

"Okay," I said, glad for the overview.

"Caleb, you can go upstairs now. I'll handle Jocelyn," Jessica told Caleb in a clipped tone.

"Jacey," I corrected her with a smile.

Jessica's eyes narrowed on me. "J.C.? As in Jocelyn Collins? What are you, a rap star?"

"N-No, ma'am..." I stuttered. "It's actually just a shortening of Jocelyn. J-A-C-E-Y."

Jessica snorted. "That's no way to start out in business. You are

Jocelyn here. Besides, you'll be working with Lacy. Lacy and Jacey sounds like the name of a flower shop."

I wondered what was so terrible about a flower shop, but I just nodded. "Yes, ma'am."

"Jessica," Jessica corrected me. "Caleb, were you planning on getting to work anytime soon?"

"Sorry." Caleb gave me a sympathetic look, then scurried off to the elevator.

I swallowed, left alone with Miss Congeniality.

Jessica got me a visitor's pass and explained some of the features of the building but quickly brought me up to the 150th floor. There, I saw a perky woman with blonde hair, blue eyes, who was pleasantly plump sitting behind a long, fogged glass reception desk.

"Lacy, this is Jocelyn Collins. Jocelyn, Lacy Everson. I have some work to do downstairs, so I'll leave you to it. Lacy is very proficient and will have you set up in no time," Jessica said.

I could have fainted with relief. Miss Congeniality was leaving.

With some clipped clicking on the floor, and the ding and swoop of the elevator doors, Jessica was gone.

Lacy bounced out from behind the desk and shook my hand. "It's so great to have some help! I've been swamped for months. Ever since Mr. Masterson's last assistant left."

I liked Lacy right away. "I'm happy to help," I replied honestly.

"Great! Now, first of all, are you really Jocelyn? That's not what Caleb calls you," Lacy said with a wink.

"Miss Congeni-er-Jessica thought Jacey was unprofessional," I responded with a wince.

"Lacy and Jacey. I like it," Lacy decided. "Come on over. I'll get you set up on your workstation, and then we can start slogging through all the backed up paperwork and mail and stuff. By the time you leave for school, we'll be current, and Caleb will know the ropes."

I nodded and sat down. For the rest of the morning, Lacy got me set up in the various systems I would need to use and the processes I would need to perform. My mind was exploding by the time lunch rolled around.

"I'd ask you to lunch, but I'll bet you're eating with Caleb. He seems like a great big brother. Is he single?" Lacy asked.

I blushed. "Um... he's my stepbrother. My parents got married when I was thirteen, and he was seventeen. So we ended up spending a lot of time together and... stuff... and then one thing led to another..."

Lacy's mouth formed an O of surprise. "You're dating your stepbrother!"

I cringed. Her voice really carried. I looked around and, sure enough, heads had popped up from their desks like meerkats. "Yes."

"Oh, girl, I am *so* jealous," Lacy continued and I relaxed fractionally. At least she hadn't said it was gross. "What a hunk of man meat."

"Uh... yeah..." I hesitantly agreed.

"Well, you get going." Lacy gave me a laughing little shove in Caleb's direction. "But just so you know, there are cameras all over the place in this building. Except in the bathrooms. So, no after hours desk sex."

I blushed to the roots of my hair. "No. Wasn't even thinking about it."

"Girl, you have something like *that* on the line and you didn't even *think* about it?" Lacy gaped.

"Uh... no?" I said.

"We've got to work on your imagination. You two have fun," Lacy giggled with a wide smile when Caleb came over.

Caleb slipped his arm around my waist, and we headed toward the elevator. "There's a nice sandwich shop downstairs," he told me. "We can get lunch there. My treat."

"It's a paid internship," I reminded him.

Caleb shrugged. "I'm still getting paid more."

With a sigh, I leaned my head on his shoulder. "I suppose I can't argue that point."

We went down to the sandwich shop. I smiled when we both got salami on Italian bread with provolone cheese, lettuce, and mayo.

Caleb picked up a soda while I went for water, though. I supposed we had to be different in some ways. That's what kept things interesting.

"What was all that about this morning when we got to the building?" I asked Caleb once we were sitting down.

"What was all what?" Caleb responded, taking a bite of his sandwich.

"You were looking at someone. And you didn't seem happy about it," I said.

Caleb grimaced and put the sandwich down. "It was the FBI," he informed me in a low tone.

"The FBI?!" I hissed back.

Caleb gestured for me to keep my voice down. "They tried to recruit me to spy on Mr. Masterson and his business, but I said no. I didn't want them trying it with you."

"Oh. Good plan," I replied. "I think we've had quite enough of law enforcement. And I'd rather not be dumped in a barrel in the middle of Lake Superior for getting caught spying."

"Exactly." We both picked up our sandwiches and ate.

Back upstairs, Mr. Masterson was standing at the front desk, chatting with Lacy. Caleb squeezed my hand, but I gave him a double-squeeze back to let him know it was all right.

Caleb reluctantly let go.

"Jacey. Caleb. How nice to see you," Mr. Masterson smiled.

"It's... nice to see you again, Mr. Masterson," I said.

"I wonder if you might accompany me to my office, Jacey," Mr. Masterson requested. "There's just some paperwork and things I think you can help with."

"I'll go," Caleb interrupted quickly. "I am your assistant, after all."

Mr. Masterson laughed and shook his head. "I like the initiative, Caleb, but I'm sure Jacey can handle this."

Caleb's lips pressed into a thin line. "I'll be at my desk." He gave me one last look, then started toward the desk outside the two big wooden double-doors to our left.

"You just come after you've put your things away," Mr. Masterson said and walked the same way.

As I was tucking my purse under my desk, Lacy leaned in. "Just lay back and enjoy it," she whispered quickly. "The money's good."

I turned to her and paled. "Excuse me?"

"And don't tell Caleb. That will just cause problems between you," Lacy said.

"Are you... are you saying what I think you're saying?" I asked.

Lacy nodded. "The money's good. Just remember that, okay? You don't want to lose this gig. Mr. Masterson can make it so you never work anywhere ever again. I've seen it happen."

I swallowed and looked at Caleb. God, what was I going to do?

"Or worse," Lacy said, dropping her voice even lower and giving a shiver.

Worse? There was something worse than...

"I-I can't!" I gasped. "Caleb's the only man I've ever been with, and I want it to stay that way."

"Then girl, you're both in trouble," Lacy responded. "You go ahead and go tell the boss that, though. He's waiting."

I took a few deep breaths then squared my shoulders. Mr. Masterson was not going to mess with me, I told myself. I wasn't going to let him.

Caleb gave me a worried look as I passed his desk, but I forced a smile. I walked through the wooden double doors with my head held high.

"I'm sure Lacy told you the deal," Mr. Masterson said from behind his desk.

"Yes. And I'm here to tell you no amount of money will get you in my pants," I replied firmly.

Mr. Masterson chuckled. "I highly doubt that. But I had a feeling that's what you'd say. So I have a different deal for you."

I frowned at him, suspicious. "What deal?"

"Let me cum on your tits, and I won't have Caleb beaten down for talking to the FBI," Mr. Masterson said.

My frown turned to a scowl. "He didn't, and you know it."

"Do I? I think I should interrogate him, just to be sure," Mr. Masterson grinned.

My breath came in angry little puffs. "You're disgusting," I said.

"Come on over here. I'm ready." Mr. Masterson showed me his hand glistening with precum.

I thought for a moment. I knew Caleb would rather take a beating than allow another man to touch me.

And since I'd never be able to keep it a secret from Caleb even if I wanted to, I sent up a silent apology to him, turned on my heel, and walked out of Mr. Masterson's office.

"You're making a mistake," Mr. Masterson called out behind me.

"No," I responded. "I'm not." I pushed the doors open and strode out.

Caleb was up and around his desk in seconds. "Jacey. Your face is all flushed. What happened?"

"That monster just–" I began.

"Caleb!" Mr. Masterson shouted. "Get in here right now! Jacey, you may go back to your station."

I swallowed and touched Caleb's cheek. "I'm sorry."

"For what?" Caleb asked.

"CALEB!!" Mr. Masterson bellowed.

I gave Caleb a kiss, then trudged back to the front desk.

"What's he going to do?" Lacy asked as I sank into my chair, shellshocked.

I whispered. "He's going to hurt Caleb."

Lacy shook her head and gave me a sympathetic look. "I told you there were worse things."

I shrugged. "If I'd done it, Caleb would have killed him. That would be a worse, worse thing."

"True." Lacy handed me a box of tissues as I started to cry.

I gave her a grateful nod and looked toward the wooden double doors. They were probably soundproofed as well.

What was happening to Caleb in there?

20

NOTHING TO LOSE

-Caleb-

I stepped into Mr. Masterson's office and folded my arms, my heart pounding with anger and fear. "What did you do to Jacey?"

Mr. Masterson snorted. "Nothing. Not for lack of trying. Your sister is a poor negotiator."

"Stepsister." I corrected him automatically. "And what was it you were *trying* to do to Jacey?"

"What do you think?" Mr. Masterson asked.

"I think you tried to fuck her," I growled.

Mr. Masterson chuckled. "I did. I did indeed try to fuck her."

It was official. I was going to kill this man.

"Don't get your panties in a wad just yet," Mr. Masterson said, holding up a hand. "She refused my offer, and I'm not into rape. So I have to make good on my promise instead."

"What promise?" I asked, infinitely relieved that Jacey hadn't been harmed.

The doors opened, admitting two of the most muscular men I'd ever seen in my life. One cracked his knuckles while the door shut and locked behind them.

Ah. So that's why she was sorry. I smiled then laughed. My Jacey made exactly the decision I would have made. Good girl.

"I don't know why you're laughing. You're about to get the worst beating you've ever had in your life," Mr. Masterson said.

"Best decision my girl ever made," I cackled. I wasn't sure exactly why I kept laughing. Maybe stress. But it was weirding out the three men in the room, and that was a good enough reason for me.

"Butch." Mr. Masterson indicated the larger of the two men. "You may begin. Toby, hold him."

I didn't resist. Not one second. Butch did indeed give me the beating of my life in places that couldn't be seen under clothing. I was sure I was going to piss blood when this was over, but it was worth it. So worth it.

After they were finished, Toby dropped me to the floor, and I threw up. Blood mixed with salami. Yum.

Mr. Masterson gave the floor a disgusted glance. "Clean that up before you leave," he said to me. "Supplies are in that closet."

It took everything in me to get to my feet, and I couldn't suppress a groan when I took my first step, but I made myself walk to the closet. I didn't want to be in this room any longer than necessary.

After scrubbing the floor clean, Mr. Masterson nodded. "Go back to your desk. I sent some spreadsheets to you for your review. I expect you to be finished by the end of the day."

"Yes, Mr. Masterson," I wheezed. I still walked out with my head held high when Mr. Masterson's goons held the doors open for me.

Jacey stood as though she were about to fly to my side, but I shook my head at her and gave her a thumbs up.

She still looked worried, but she sat back down.

I sank down into my office chair and started to get to work.

***

IT WAS night by the time I finished all the work Mr. Masterson had given me. I looked around for Jacey and saw she was still at the reception desk, watching me.

I picked up my suit jacket and went to the reception desk. "Hey, baby," I said. "Ready to go home?"

Jacey nodded and took my hand. She tried to cuddle into my side, but I hissed in pain.

She jumped back. "Caleb, what did they do to you?"

"Nothing some ice and a good night's sleep can't fix," I replied, taking her hand again. "I'm proud of you."

Jacey stared at the floor, sniffling. "All he wanted was to cum on my boobs. I should have let him."

"Um, no, you shouldn't have," I said firmly. "The only cum getting on those tits is going to be mine."

Looking back up at me, Jacey asked, "So you think it was worth it?"

"So worth it," I responded. I kissed her. "Let's go home so we can play sexy nurse and patient."

Jacey gave a wet laugh. "You're incorrigible."

"I am. I know it." We got into the elevator.

The doors were closing when a beefy hand reached out and stopped them.

I tensed and put Jacey behind me.

Toby and Butch were standing there, stone-faced.

"What do you want?" I asked angrily.

"Boss says we're to give the girl a beat-down," Butch said. "Doesn't think you learned your lesson."

I backed to the wall with Jacey behind me. "Not going to happen. Not while I'm alive."

"The boss wasn't particular on that point, either," Butch shrugged.

"Oh my God," Jacey gasped.

"Listen, you two meatheads, I'm leaving the office now. With Jacey. Mr. Masterson is just going to have to accept that," I growled.

In response, Butch muscled his way into the elevator. I threw a good punch or two, and he'd be feeling those in the morning, but ultimately Butch overpowered me and held me so Tony could zip-tie my wrists and ankles.

Butch then cocked his head at Jacey. "You gonna give me any trouble?"

"I'll go with you," Jacey said. "Just don't hurt Caleb."

"Fair deal." Toby slung me over his shoulder while Butch escorted Jacey behind us back to Mr. Masterson's office.

Mr. Masterson greeted us with a smile. "That was very good work you did today, Caleb. I'm quite pleased."

"So you're tying me up because I did good work?" I spat.

"No. I'm tying you up because I want you to understand something." Mr. Masterson took a gun out of his desk and pointed it right at Jacey. "You belong to me. If you breathe, that's a breath I allowed you to have. Your lives are now mine."

I swallowed any sarcastic response I might have had. "Please leave Jacey alone."

"I will. On one condition," Mr. Masterson said.

"Am I going to like the condition?" I asked warily.

"You're not in a position to argue it. And no, you're not going to like it. You're going to loathe it. But it's my price." Mr. Masterson steepled his fingers under his chin. "As a beating didn't seem to teach you anything."

"I learned plenty. I promise. I did all that work you gave me without complaining, remember?" I argued.

Mr. Masterson shook his head. "No. I don't think you did. So, my condition for allowing you to live today—"

"I won't fuck you. You'll have to kill me," Jacey said firmly.

"Me, too," I added.

"Yes, yes, we've been over that. I liked watching you at my house. I've decided I'd like to watch a live show," Mr. Masterson grinned.

"Oh fuck no," I said right away.

Jacey shook her head slowly. "I won't."

"Even under threat of death?" Mr. Masterson asked, raising his eyebrows. "You'd just come in here on your lunches and—"

"What, you'd even want us to do it every day? Pass," I cut in.

"So you would do it once?" Mr. Masterson smirked at us.

I had a dark feeling that once was going to turn into twice, and then before we knew it, we'd be putting on a show for this bastard three times a day, every day.

Mr. Masterson turned the gun on me. "Would you do it once?"

Jacey paled. "Don't hurt him."

"I could beat him down every day, Jacey. Is one little public fuck worth that?" Mr. Masterson asked.

"I'll do it. I'll do it, just leave Caleb alone," Jacey begged.

"Jacey..." I murmured a warning.

Jacey turned to me. "Please, Caleb? Just once."

My nostrils flared as anger took over my whole body. But Jacey was asking now, and I'd never been able to deny her anything.

"Fine," I conceded. "But not today. You beat me so bad I'm not sure I physically can."

Mr. Masterson regarded us a while, then nodded. He put the gun away. "I'll give Caleb time to heal."

"What, no conditions?" I grunted.

"No. I think I've pushed you as far as you'll go. Today," Mr. Masterson added with a smirk.

I could see where this road was leading. Ultimately, that man intended to fuck my Jacey.

Toby put me down and cut the zip ties. I took Jacey's hand and nearly ran from the office, dragging her behind me.

"Caleb. Caleb!" Jacey said, breathless as we boarded the elevator.

My heart stopped pounding in my ears when, blessedly, the elevator doors closed behind us. "What is it?" I asked.

"What are we going to do?" Jacey clung to my arm. "We can't just let him watch us."

"He wants to do more than watch, and eventually he's going to wear us down, in little baby steps," I told her. "I'm not going to let that happen."

"So... again I ask, what are we going to do?" Jacey inquired.

"I'll show you." We walked out of the building and to my car.

We got in, then I drove us to a supermarket and picked up two burner phones. When we got back into the car, I handed one to Jacey.

Then I took the stiff business card out of my pocket and dialed.

"Church," came the clipped answer.

"This is Caleb Killeen. We're in," I said without preamble.

"Meet me at Jake's Diner. We'll talk there," Darren replied, also not wasting words.

"We'll be there." I hung up the phone.

Jacey looked from her burner phone, to me, and back again. "What exactly are we doing?"

"Helping the FBI," I replied.

"Oh. Oh dear," Jacey mumbled.

"It's our one chance," I said. "The only way through this is to take that bastard down."

Jacey leaned her head against my shoulder. "But we hate the authorities."

"We do," I agreed.

"And this is going to be very, very dangerous," Jacey pointed out.

"It's going to be worth it. I'm going to do this or die trying. I'm not going to let Masterson hurt you," I stated.

Jacey looked up at me with wide green eyes. "I don't want him to hurt you, either."

"Then let's do this," I said.

"Okay," Jacey replied.

I put the car in gear, and we headed to Jake's Diner.

INSIDE, the diner was nearly deserted. I wondered if that was by design.

Darren was sitting in a corner booth, nursing a cup of coffee. "Caleb. Jacey. Go ahead and sit down."

We sat down across from him. I winced at the movement.

"So you've changed your minds," Darren observed.

"First of all, Jacey and I need some sort of escape plan. If we need to pull out fast, you'll be able to get us out fast." I ticked my points off on my fingers. "Second of all, if something happens to me, you're going to take care of Jacey. Get her out. Put her in witness protection. Third, we're going into witness protection after this. No more of this going from agency to agency to see what kind of mileage you can get out of us. After this, we're done. You understand?"

"Perfectly," Darren said. "I'll bring your demands to my superiors."

A waitress approached, and Jacey jumped.

"Oh dear, honey. Rough day?" the waitress asked.

"Very," I replied for her. "Could we get two slices of that apple pie with some ice cream? Thanks."

"Anything to drink?" the waitress asked.

"Just water, thanks," I answered.

As the waitress walked away, Jacey took several deep breaths and buried her face in my shoulder.

"I want an agreement in writing before Jacey or I do anything," I informed Darren. "In writing. Signed documents."

"I'll have to run it up the flagpole, but your requests are not unreasonable," Darren said.

Jacey popped her head up. "The same goes for Caleb."

"What goes for Caleb?" Darren asked.

"If something happens to me, you take care of Caleb," Jacey insisted.

I wanted to tell her nothing would happen to her. But we didn't tell each other lies, and there was no sugar coating here.

"What made you decide to help us?" Darren looked back and forth between Jacey and me.

"It's very simple," I replied. "We have nothing to lose."

21
____

IT'S MY LIFE

-Jacey-

"Baby, get in with me?" Caleb asked once I had him in a warm bath. His abdomen looked awful, and there was also bruising on his arms and legs.

"Why?" I eyed him suspiciously.

Caleb gestured to his rigid dick.

"Caleb," I scolded him. "You're hurt. I'm surprised you can even get it up at all. If I get in there, it's just going to hurt you."

Caleb pouted. "It's your fault."

"How is it my fault?" I demanded.

"You're all sexy when you wash me," Caleb grinned.

I rolled my eyes. "Caleb, I was washing you. Just washing you. Not sexy-time washing you. Now you just sit there and soak."

"Fine. We'll do it in bed. I'll lay on my back and let you do all the work," Caleb said.

"No. That's my final answer. You need to get better first," I replied.

Caleb sighed. "How long will that be?"

"A few days at least, I think. I don't know. You're the one who studied medicine," I pointed out.

"Hmm." Caleb stroked his fingertips down my arm as I leaned on the edge of the tub. "We are going to sleep together, though, right?'

I smiled and stroked his hair. "Of course. I wouldn't be anywhere else."

"Good," Caleb said.

In truth, I was worried about his nightmares. Otherwise, I might have slept in my own bed. I didn't want to bump his bruises during the night.

After about half an hour, I helped Caleb out of the tub. I patted him dry very gently, then we walked into his bedroom.

I stripped out of habit. Caleb got into bed, and I could see the spark of desire in his eyes.

"I'll go put on some pajamas," I said, starting for my bedroom.

"No. Don't," Caleb replied. He held out his hand to me. "Just come to bed. I'll be good, I promise."

I laughed in disbelief. "Yeah, right."

"I promise," Caleb said again.

I sighed. He sounded so down.

"You'd better be good," I grumbled and crawled into bed with him, stark naked.

Caleb spooned me from behind and wrapped his arm around me. He kissed the back of my neck. "Good night baby."

"Good night, Caleb," I responded.

I DREAMED ABOUT MR. MASTERSON.

His hands were all over me. In fact, it was as though he had more than one pair.

He held me down on top of his desk and kicked my legs apart.

"Let's make a deal," he said, and kept saying it. "Let's make a deal. Let's make a deal."

I struggled, but I couldn't get away.

"No!" I screamed when he entered me. "No! No!"

Mr. Masterson just laughed. "Let's make a deal. Let's make a deal."

"Jacey."

I heard Caleb's voice, but I couldn't see him. I cried out desperately. "Caleb!"

"Jacey, baby, wake up. I'm here. I'm right here."

My eyes flew open, and I saw Caleb leaning over me, looking concerned. My whole body had broken out in a cold sweat.

"Caleb," I sobbed and wrapped my arms around his neck.

"Hey, baby. Everything's okay. I'm here," Caleb whispered, wrapping me in his arms.

"What's that racket?!" my father shouted outside the door.

"Nightmare, Dad. Go back to sleep," I called back.

There was a pause, then my father asked, "Jacey, what are you doing in Caleb's room?"

"It... it was the nightmare... I came in after the nightmare..." I invented quickly.

"Well, get to bed. We all have to work in the morning," my father grumbled.

We listened to him pad back down the hall, then Caleb turned to me. "Baby, what happened? What were you dreaming about?"

"I..." my voice hitched. "I dreamed Mr. Masterson was raping me."

Caleb swore and held me tighter. "I'm sorry, baby. I'm so sorry."

I knew it must hurt him to be holding me this way, but I couldn't seem to let go. "I... I..."

"What is it, baby?" Caleb asked, rocking me. "You can tell me."

I couldn't. It wasn't right. Not while Caleb was in this condition.

Caleb put his lips right by my ear. "Do you want me to make love to you, baby?"

With a sniffle, I nodded my head.

Caleb laid me down gently, kissing me.

Then it was his hands roaming over my body. His rough, familiar palms touching my breasts and belly.

Kissing me again, Caleb pressed his fingers up into me. I whimpered.

"Don't worry, baby. I'll get you wet," Caleb assured me. He moved his fingers very slowly inside me and thumbed my clit, licking and sucking my nipples.

True to his word, Caleb worked me until I was dripping for him. "Caleb. Please. I want you inside me now," I murmured when I thought he might make me climax on his hand. I didn't want that. I wanted to climax on his cock.

Caleb removed his fingers and spread some of my juices along his shaft. Then he moved over me. "A little bit wider, baby. There we go."

Once I widened my legs, Caleb pressed the head of his dick against my entrance, then thrust gently inside, all the way to the hilt.

"Caleb," I sighed, looping my arms around his neck. "Does it... hurt to do this?"

"It's worth it. Trust me," Caleb said. He kissed me, pulling back a little, then thrusting in again.

He was slow and gentle with me, and it was so beautiful it made me cry. Caleb kissed my tears and kept moving, touching me everywhere until all there was in my world was Caleb.

We came together, our bodies straining for each other, and Caleb groaned against my shoulder as he filled me with his warm seed.

"What the FUCK is going on here?!" my father bellowed.

I looked up and saw Caleb's door was open, my father holding the key.

Caleb swore and pulled the covers over us, protecting my naked body from my father's eyes. "What does it look like?" Caleb snapped. "Jesus, could you knock?!"

"Are you... are you fucking your sister? Jacey, are you fucking your brother?! Answer me!" my father demanded, spittle flying from his lips.

Jeanie appeared then. "Oh dear," was all she said.

"She is *not* my sister!" Caleb replied, exasperated.

"She is your sister!" my father insisted. "Jesus. Jesus Christ!"

I clung to Caleb, looking at my father and Jeanie, not sure exactly what to do. That my father had found us out was a tragedy. I had no idea what he was going to do.

"Get off her, boy. Right now," my father growled.

"Not a chance," Caleb responded. "You're the one who interrupted us."

"Of course I interrupted you, you are FUCKING YOUR SISTER!!" my father all but screamed.

"Dad, it's okay. Caleb and I love each other very much," I tried to explain.

My father was having none of it. He stormed into the bedroom and grabbed Caleb by his bare, bruised shoulder.

Caleb hissed and pulled out of me. He slid out from under the comforter, careful to make sure I was still covered, then rounded on my father. "This is a huge invasion of our privacy."

"Your privacy?! That's my daughter you're dipping your dick into!" my father yelled.

"Hank, the neighbors are going to hear," Jeanie said softly.

"Then let them hear this." My father hauled back and punched Caleb in the face.

"No!" I cried.

Caleb's head snapped back. But he wasn't down for the count. He punched my father right back, hard enough to knock him backward into the dresser and shatter the mirror.

My dad wiped the blood off his lip while Caleb bled from his nose.

"Both of you, stop!" Jeanie shouted.

They didn't stop. My father stood up to face Caleb again. He took a few swings, which Caleb dodged this time.

"You leave my little girl alone, do you hear me?!" my father snarled.

"No," Caleb responded simply.

"What the FUCK do you think you're doing?!" My father took another swing.

"I was making love to the woman I love until you came in," Caleb replied.

My father finally backed Caleb to the wall and took a pot shot at his abdomen.

Caleb groaned and doubled over.

"Dad, no!" I jumped out of bed and grabbed his arm when he was going to punch Caleb again.

My father threw me off him. I tripped on the comforter, which was now on the floor, and hit my head on the bedside table.

Jeanie gasped.

Caleb saw what had happened and the look of hatred in his eyes was palpable. He swung hard at my father, and there was a loud crunch.

My father stumbled back, clutching his face. Caleb hobbled to my side and helped me up.

I was bleeding from my temple. A lot.

Caleb thumbed some of the blood out of the way to take a good look. "I don't think it needs stitches. It's just a little cut. But it's a head wound, so it's going to bleed a lot."

"Get out," my father snarled while Caleb was examining me. "Boy, you get out of my house."

"Hank, no. We can work this out," Jeanie said. "They're both grown ups. And they're not biologically related..."

My father turned his glare on Jeanie. "Are you telling me this is okay with you?"

"No. Not at all," Jeanie responded. "I'm saying it's not our choice to make."

"Well, I'm making that choice. Jacey, go to your room. Caleb, pack your shit and get out of here," my father snapped.

Caleb looked at me and I nodded in silent agreement. I went to my room and pulled on some clothes, then began packing myself.

"What are you doing, Jacey?" my father asked.

"I'm leaving with Caleb," I said. I hefted my bag over my shoulder. "And if you try to keep me here again, I will press charges."

My father paled, then turned bright red. "Fine! Get out. Both of you! You disgust me!"

Caleb put his arm around me when I came back into his room then escorted me past my father and Jeanie and out to his car. "If you need us," he called out the window to my father and Jeanie. "We'll be at a motel."

Jeanie burst into tears, but my father just stood there with his arms folded, a look of deep betrayal on his face.

I would never forget that look.

Tears streamed down my cheeks, and Caleb took my hand in his. "It's okay," he said. "It's going to be okay."

Considering all the shit we were in with Masterson and the fact that our parents were 'disgusted' by us, I was beginning to doubt it. "Do we even have enough money for a motel?" I asked glumly.

"I do." Caleb squeezed my hand. "I got a bonus for agreeing to work there in the first place. Apparently, it's something they give all the assistants."

"Oh. Okay." We were okay on the finding shelter part, at least. I looked out the window into the darkness at the yellow and white lines that seemed to go on forever as we entered farm country.

"What if we just kept going?" I whispered.

"Going?" Caleb asked. "Going where?"

"Anywhere. Everywhere. Just going and going and going," I said.

Caleb looked over at me briefly. He ran his thumb over the back of my hand in a comforting manner. "I don't think we can outrun them all."

"Probably not," I sighed.

Caleb leaned over and gave my healing temple a quick kiss. "I love you, Jacey. I want us to make a life together. I don't want law enforcement and Masterson and Girard nipping at our heels. We'd never be able to stop running."

"I know. It was just a thought," I said.

"It was a nice thought," Caleb responded softly. "I'd go anywhere with you, Jacey. All around the world and back again. But I also want to see you in the yard, playing with our children someday."

I imagined pushing a little boy who looked just like Caleb on the swing set in the back of a modest white house. "I want that, too."

"Good. So we're going to take Masterson down and get our lives back?" Caleb said.

I nodded. "Yes, Caleb. We're going to get our lives back."

22

MISSION IMPOSSIBLE

-Caleb-

Instead of a motel, I actually rented a room in a hotel close to work. It was a little spendy, being in the heart of Minneapolis, but with what Masterson paid me in a sign-on bonus, I could afford it.

That meant we had a nice jacuzzi tub in the bathroom, which I sank into shortly after we arrived and soaked, letting the heat draw away the pain of my beat down from Masterson and Hank's beating.

Added bonus? This time I did convince Jacey to sit on my cock. The pleasure of being inside her drove away most of the pain.

"Baby, you feel so good," I murmured, kissing her shoulder. I freely played with her breasts while she rode me gently, moving up and down on my dick.

"You're sure this doesn't hurt too much?" Jacey asked worriedly.

"It's fine, baby. Just keep going. Yeah, just like that," I groaned. Pretty soon, I gripped Jacey's hips and started slamming her down onto me, splashing water over the side of the tub and making our bodies slap together noisily.

"Caleb!" Jacey gasped. "You're going to hurt yourself!"

"Worth it," I growled. I pinched her clit and sent her right over the edge. I followed right on the heels of her orgasm, cumming hard inside her.

When it was over, Jacey leaned forward, panting, gripping the sides of the tub. I pulled her back against me. Sure, it hurt, but I wanted her there, skin to skin.

"Caleb..." Jacey objected.

I kissed her protest away. "Shh. I'm okay."

Jacey looked uncertain, but the way I swelled up again inside her and prepared for another go seemed to convince her.

This time, I bent her over the side of the tub and took her without mercy. Jacey screamed when she came, her whole body arching back into mine.

I squeezed her breasts as I came, which made Jacey let out the sweetest little squeak.

"Caleb," Jacey panted, "we should go to bed. We still need to work tomorrow. Today."

"Sure," I replied innocently.

Once we were in bed, I had Jacey again. Twice. Then I fell asleep dick deep in her as God intended.

In the morning, I woke up to Jacey fluttering little kisses over my collarbone, neck, and cheeks. When I slitted my eyes open, she put my hand on her breast.

That was all the invitation I needed to take care of my morning wood. I rolled Jacey underneath me, and she spread her legs wide. I took her hard and fast, the sound of the alarm we set beeping about halfway through our sex.

I reached, trying to slap it while still thrusting inside Jacey. She giggled when I missed twice before finally turning the thing off.

"You think that's funny?" I grinned at her.

Jacey nodded unrepentantly.

I kissed her nose and gave her an extra hard, sharp thrust.

Jacey gasped and nearly went cross-eyed as she gripped my shoulders and came.

"That's my good girl," I groaned as she milked me dry.

We laid there a moment, Jacey staring at the closet where our work clothes were hanging. "I don't want to go in," she said softly.

"I don't either, baby," I sighed. "But I've got a feeling he'll come find us if we don't, and at least at work, there're other people around."

"A lot of good that did us yesterday," Jacey responded bitterly.

I kissed her frown. "Baby, I know you're with me, right?"

Jacey looked up at me. "I am. Always."

"Good. Now let's go have shower sex and get ready for work," I grinned.

Jacey giggled, and I pulled out so I could get out of bed and offer her my hand. Just as she took it, my burner phone rang.

I grabbed it and answered while Jacey bit her lip nervously. "Hello?" I said.

"Good news," Darren replied. "Your terms are acceptable. Meet me at the diner after work today, and we'll have you both sign the agreements. Then I can give you your assignments."

"Sounds good." I gave Jacey a thumb's up. "Whenever he lets us go, we'll be there."

"I'll be waiting," Darren said and hung up.

I went back to the bed and gave Jacey a hug. "It's done. We just have to sign."

"Good." Jacey bit her lip. "We're still making the right decision?"

"Absolutely," I replied, my voice completely free of doubt. "I don't see any other way out of this."

Jacey nodded. "Okay. Then I guess we get to be spies."

I chuckled and hummed a popular spy show theme.

Jacey swatted me. "It's not funny."

"It's a little funny." I tickled her.

Jacey laughed and wriggled. "All right! It's a little funny."

I kissed Jacey and lifted her in my arms, heading for the shower.

"Baby, we're going to write our own future. Just wait and see," I said.

WORK WAS BLESSEDLY UNEVENTFUL. Jacey and I went to lunch at the sandwich shop and continued to train on our jobs. We left at a decent hour. The only creepy part was that Mr. Masterson kept looking at me as though evaluating my fitness level for banging Jacey in his office.

I hammed up the wincing and low groans just to keep him off our backs. When five-thirty hit, I practically ran to Jacey.

"Let's get out of here," I said to her.

Jacey nodded emphatically, and we got on the elevator, holding our breath, hoping some meaty hand didn't reach in and stop it.

Luckily, the doors closed without incident. Jacey sagged against me. "I don't think this is doing anything good for our hearts," she observed.

"We'll both get EKGs when this is all over," I responded.

We ran across the busy Minneapolis street to where my car was parked and jumped in. By five-forty, I was peeling out of the parking lot and out into the suburbs to Jake's Diner.

Darren was waiting in the same booth, along with someone in a three-piece suit. Jacey and I slid into the booth across from them.

"Welcome back," Darren said. "This is state's attorney Adam Jerod. He's the one with the paperwork. I'm here to witness."

"Sounds good," I replied.

Adam snapped open a briefcase and laid a paperclipped stack of papers in front of each of us. "The initial and signature places are tabbed. But if you want to read the whole thing over, that's fine by me."

"Oh, I'm reading it over," I told him. I put an arm around Jacey, and we read my copy together, flipping through Jacey's to make sure hers was the same.

Darren was right. Everything I'd stipulated was in the agreements, plus more information about the kind of living stipends we'd get when we were in witness protection and things like that.

Jacey nodded at me after we read the last page, and Adam handed us each a pen.

In less than ten minutes, we'd signed our lives away.

"Good. Now that's done, I'll let Darren and you complete your business," Adam said and slid out of the booth.

"Thanks, Adam," Darren called absently as he left. "Let's get something to eat. Then we can go over the details."

I didn't taste my burger and I don't think Jacey did, either. But it was important to make sure we got the calories in, especially considering the active sex life Jacey and I had.

Darren leaned over the table when he finished his BLT and the dishes had been taken away. "I need evidence of Mr. Masterson's wrongdoings."

"I kind of figured," I responded dryly.

Darren frowned at me, and I went silent. "We basically want to see where the money's going. I don't think you're going to find any files with a neon flashing sign that says, 'Look here, illegal logging!' But if I could get a copy of his real financial records, our forensic accountants can take it from there."

Jacey looked at me. "Well... I was actually sort of hoping there would be files about his illegal logging activities."

"He won't make it that easy." Darren grimaced. "We've been trying to nail this scumbag for three years now. He doesn't make anything easy."

"Tell me about it," I muttered.

Darren's eyes narrowed on me. "You're pretty bruised up there, buddy."

"You should see what's under the clothes. I had to tell everyone at work I fell down some stairs," I said.

"What really happened?" Darren asked.

"Masterson got angry because Jacey won't have sex with him and decided to beat me down as a kind of punishment. Then Jacey's dad walked in on us while we were making love and figured out that I'm screwing his daughter. He wasn't really happy about it," I replied.

Darren snorted. "Doesn't look like he was."

"Mr. Masterson said when Caleb's feeling better, we have to have sex in his office in front of him or he's... well, he threatened to kill us," Jacey added.

Darren's eyebrows nearly hit his hairline. "I knew he had a habit of screwing his female employees, but this is a new one."

"He had us on camera when we were living at his house, before we knew what he was," I explained. "I guess he liked what he saw."

"That's one sick bastard," Darren said.

"Yeah. And we'd like to not be under his thumb anymore," I responded.

Darren nodded. "Completely understandable. If this works out, you won't have to see him again until he's in court."

"Wait, 'if' this works out?!" I protested.

Darren shrugged. "There are no guarantees in this business. Either way, if things get too hot, we're getting you out."

"You do know the last person who 'got us out' of anything was shot dead, right?" Jacey asked.

"Really." Darren took out a notepad and began scribbling. "You witnessed it?"

"Yes. It was a Canadian detective," I said.

Darren paused, then prompted, "You got a name?"

"Dick," Jacey remembered, and I nodded my agreement. "His colleague who brought us to the states called him Dick."

"Sounds like I need to liaise with the Canadians," Darren said.

I laughed bitterly. "Oh man. If you think that's something, wait until you hear the rest." Then, between us, Jacey and I told Darren the whole story of our Canadian adventures.

Darren took copious notes, shaking his head in places. "You two are the luckiest bastards I have ever met."

"I think I owe my continued existence to Jacey," I replied honestly. "Girard had a soft spot for you."

Jacey scoffed. "Girard and the men had a hard-on for me. I don't know why."

Darren looked up and looked Jacey up and down. "I do."I bared my teeth at him, but Darren waved a hand. "Not making a move. Just stating facts."

"So, now that we know what we're supposed to be looking for, can we go now?" I asked.

"You've become much more valuable witnesses in the last thirty minutes," Darren observed.

"Does that mean we can go into witness protection now?" I hoped.

Jacey grabbed my hand and squeezed, hopeful as well.

Darren sighed and shook his head. "You're also primely placed. I also had a favor to ask you."

"A favor?" I repeated. I didn't like the sound of that.

"Do you think there's any way you could get yourselves back in the Masterson mansion?" Darren asked.

Jacey's jaw dropped.

I was pretty sure mine did the same thing. "You've got to be kidding me."

"You said you were friends with his son," Darren pointed out.

"Yeah. Was. He was watching Jacey and I have sex," I said.

"It might kill two birds with one stone. He gets to see you fuck, so you don't have to do it at the office. And you get access to more sensitive information," Darren replied.

I ground my teeth. "You make a good point. You'd think you convinced people to do things they didn't want to do for a living."

Darren chuckled. "You'd think."

Jacey bit her lip, then said, "I suppose we could try."

"Yeah," I agreed. "I suppose we could try."

23

INTO THE LION'S DEN

-Jacey-

Caleb used his own cell phone to call Will.

"Yeah," Caleb said gruffly. "Hank kicked us out. He found out about us."

Will was loud enough that I could hear his side of the conversation. "Dude, I never thought you'd call me again."

"Yeah, well, we're working for your dad now. You probably know that already. I thought maybe we might as well just go back and live with you, with what he's demanding. He's a demanding kind of guy." I knew Caleb didn't have to fake the anger in his tone.

"He wants to watch you fuck Jacey," Will said without doubt.

"Good guess," Caleb snorted.

"I didn't have to guess," was Will's reply. He actually sounded sad. "Yeah, sure, come on back. I'll make sure your room's in order."

"Thanks." Caleb hung up the phone.

We drove from Jake's Diner straight to the hotel, then to Minnetonka and up to the gates of the Masterson mansion. We were let in immediately.

Will was waiting for us on the front steps. "Here, Chris will park your car."

Caleb handed Will the keys, and Will tossed them to a man behind him who dutifully walked over to the Prius and drove it away.

"I guess we'll just get settled," Caleb grunted.

"Hey, man," Will said, catching Caleb's arm. "I'm sorry. I really am. I know what it's like to be... under his control."

Caleb softened then. He clasped hands with Will. "I figure if anyone knew, it would be his son."

Will swallowed and nodded.

Caleb put a hand on my back, and we walked straight to the room we'd shared before. It was set up like before, with energy drinks and power bars. The only difference was there was a chair in the corner. And in it was Mr. Masterson.

"Welcome back," he said with a wide, lascivious smile. "I've decided you can take the next two days off work. I have a proposal for you."

I gripped Caleb's arm. Dear God, another proposal?!

"I want you to get your IUD removed, Jacey." How he knew I had an IUD was anyone's guess, but it really grossed me out.

"Wh-Why?" I asked.

"Yeah, why?" Caleb echoed.

Mr. Masterson smirked. "Will needs to start doing his duties as my son. One of those duties is to produce an heir, as I'm sure you can guess."

He didn't need to say the rest. "No," Caleb and I said together.

"You haven't even heard the sweet part of the deal," Mr. Masterson responded.

"We don't have to," Caleb hissed. "Now, if you want to watch us fuck, fine. But I'm not going to let you use Jacey as some kind of incubator."

I could have cheered. "That's right!" I said.

"If you do this, I'll give you what you want," Mr. Masterson went on as though we hadn't said anything.

"We don't care-" Caleb snapped.

"Your freedom," Mr. Masterson interrupted. "I won't even chase you for talking to the FBI."

Every drop of blood I had suddenly rushed to my toes. "What?" I whispered.

"You think I don't keep tabs. Though, points for the burner phone, Caleb. Nice touch," Mr. Masterson chuckled.

I was going to be sick.

Caleb stood in front of me. "I convinced her to do it. If you want to punish someone, punish me."

"I will be punishing you. You'll have to watch as Jacey 'incubates' another man's child," Mr. Masterson said sweetly.

"No," I gasped. "Oh, God, no."

"Don't worry. It can all be done clinically. I'm not going to force you to have sex with Will," Mr. Masterson continued.

I gripped Caleb's arm so I didn't faint. Fainting would not be the united show of strength we were going for.

"We said no," Caleb gritted out.

Mr. Masterson clucked his tongue. "That's too bad."

I braced myself for whatever punishment Mr. Masterson was going to mete out on Caleb.

Instead, Mr. Masterson just raised a gun.

"No!" I shouted. "Don't kill-!"

Mr. Masterson shot Caleb in the leg. I cried out, then we both looked down and saw it was some kind of dart.

"You sonofa..." Caleb weaved and fell to the floor.

I turned to the door and started to run, but I felt a sting in my ass.

The last thing I remembered was reaching for the doorknob.

I don't think I made it that far.

WHEN I WOKE UP, it was early morning, and I was sore. I felt as though I'd been stabbed in the ass multiple times.

I was on the bed in the room I shared with Caleb, but Caleb wasn't here. I was naked under a hospital gown. I panicked. "Caleb?!"

The door swung open, and Will came in with a tray. "You're awake," he said solemnly.

"Where's Caleb? Is he okay?!" I demanded.

Will set down the tray and sat down in the chair Mr. Masterson had once occupied. "Caleb is fine. He's locked in a different room."

"Why?" I asked.

"Because the doctor was performing the procedures in here," Will said glumly.

Procedures? I gaped at Will. "What procedures?"

"Jacey... you've been out about three months," Will replied with a swallow. "And you're pregnant. And it's mine."

Every point he made was a stab to my heart. I felt tears creeping down my cheeks, but I dashed them away. "I want Caleb."

"I know. I'll have him brought here," Will said. "I made sure they didn't hurt him, Jacey."

I didn't know whether to thank him or claw his eyes out. Maybe rip off his balls. "Go away, Will."

"I'm sorry-" Will started.

"You say that a lot," I muttered. "Just go away."

Will nodded sadly and stood. He walked to the door, hesitated as though he wanted to say something more, then shook his head and kept going.

The next time the door opened, Caleb was there. He had raccoon eyes, as though he hadn't slept the entire three months he was away from me.

I hiccuped and opened my arms to him.

Caleb came straight to the bed and wrapped me in his arms, burying his face in my hair. "Jacey..." he murmured. He kissed me all over my face. "Jacey."

The door shut and locked behind him.

I burst into tears. "I'm pregnant."

"I know," Caleb said.

"It's Will's," I choked out.

"I know," Caleb repeated.

I tried to bite it back, but I let out a sob just the same. "What are we going to do?"

Caleb kissed me and held me tightly. "I don't know. Baby, I don't know."

"I thought we were going to get out," I whispered. "I thought... I thought this would all be over soon."

"It was my mistake," Caleb bit out. "Mine. I'm so sorry."

I shook my head. "He'd have come up with this eventually. And... he did say if I have Will's baby, he'll let us go and live our lives."

"Do you believe him?" Caleb asked in a tone that suggested he did not.

"No," I whispered. "I don't."

Caleb stroked my hair away from my face. "Do you hurt?"

I nodded. "I-I think they gave me hormones and whatever else they do."

"Oh my sweet baby." Caleb's words were strained. It was then I figured out he was crying as well.

I cuddled closer to Caleb and rubbed his back. "We'll come up with something. We always do."

"And look where that's got us," Caleb replied bitterly.

Tears spilled down my cheeks once more. "Please, Caleb. Please don't lose hope. Please don't leave me alone."

"I will never leave you alone," Caleb promised. He kissed my forehead. "No matter what happens."

"Thank you," I said softly.

"For what?" Caleb asked.

"Being here. Being you." I kissed him and pushed him onto his back. I needed to be close with him. I was desperate for it.

"Jacey?" Caleb frowned as I started to undo his pants. He stopped my hands.

I hiccuped another sob. "Do you not want me anymore?"

"Not w-of course, I want you," Caleb replied. "But you said you hurt."

"I'm just a little sore." Our tears mixed together as I kissed him. "Please, Caleb? Please?"

Caleb's brow furrowed. "I just don't know-"

"For me," I begged. "I need to feel you."

Caleb gave in with a sigh and a nod. The hands that had stopped me before helped me open his pants and shove them down.

I reached behind me and undid the ties of the hospital gown, letting it fall away.

Caleb looked stricken. "That's all they gave you to wear?"

"I only just woke up today. I suppose it helped with the procedures," I responded with a shudder.

Caleb rolled so I was under him. "I think maybe I should do the work this time, baby. Three months under. Jesus."

"If I was ever up, I don't remember. They drugged me." I looped my arms around Caleb's neck as he moved over me.

He had to stroke himself hard, I noticed. He'd never had to do that before. My spirits fell. Maybe he really didn't want me as much now that I was carrying Will's child.

As though reading my mind, Caleb said, "Baby, I just don't like the idea we're doing this on camera for Mr. Masterson's pleasure. It has nothing to do with how much I want you."

I blushed at my own insecurity. "Sorry."

"Don't be sorry." Caleb kissed my tears. "Don't ever be sorry." He palmed my breasts.

I nearly jumped.

Caleb stopped. "What's wrong?"

"They're just... really sensitive," I answered.

"Really?" Caleb dropped his head and gently licked, then sucked on a nipple.

I groaned. I could have come from that contact alone. "Caleb. Caleb, you have to be in me now. You're going to make me come."

"You're damn right I am," Caleb grunted. The head of his cock lined up with my entrance, and he slowly began to push inside.

I cried out. It hurt. But I wanted it. I wanted him inside me.

Caleb let out a strained breath. "Are you sure this is okay?"

"Yes," I replied. "Please. More."

Caleb slid the rest of the way in, playing with my breasts the whole time, tugging expertly at my nipples.

I shattered. There was no other word for it. I felt my whole being come apart as I came around the man I loved, carrying the baby of a man I didn't. I clung to Caleb and sobbed.

He rocked me and whispered reassurances we both knew might not end up being true. It took me a moment to realize Caleb hadn't come. In fact, he'd gone soft.

"Caleb?" I asked, my insecurities rising again.

Caleb pointed.

Will was standing in the doorway.

I yipped and Caleb yanked the sheets up. "You, too?" Caleb accused.

"No. Really. Sorry. I didn't see that much," Will said, blushing scarlet.

"What do you want, Will, if it's not to get your jollies?" Caleb asked.

Will looked at me. Then he walked to the bed, took my hand, and placed something in it.

I looked down. It was a thumb drive.

"You've got fifteen minutes. Get dressed and go," Will said urgently.

Caleb didn't have to be told twice. He was out me, off the bed, and yanking on his clothes in seconds.

I stared up at Will. "Will, what is this?"

"What you need," Will replied. He swallowed. "Please take care of the baby. I know Caleb will be a good dad."

"Will...?" I breathed.

"Go." Will stepped out of the room. I could hear him walking quickly down the hall.

"Jacey." Caleb tossed me my pants and a shirt. "We've got to get out of here."

I threw off the covers and pulled my own clothes on.

Then Caleb was tugging me down the hall to the front door.

Chris was standing there by the Prius, dangling Caleb's keys.

Caleb snatched them.

"Good luck," Chris said. "From all of us."

Caleb put me in the passenger seat and gently buckled me in like he usually did. He came around the other side, slammed his buckle into place, and put the pedal to the floor.

The gate scraped the sides of the Prius as it started to close.

"Where do we go now?" I asked, gripping the oh-shit bar as Caleb sped down the road.

"I don't know," Caleb said. "I honestly don't know."

24

───────────

GETTING OUT

-Caleb-

I knew we had to ditch the Prius. There was no way Mr. Masterson wasn't tracking it.

"We'll drive to Wisconsin and then stop at a rental car agency," I invented wildly while we sped down the road. "Then we'll ditch the Prius and just keep driving until we get to Washington D.C. or something. I don't know. Some FBI office."

"Okay," Jacey agreed, clutching her seatbelt and the oh-shit bar. "Okay."

I nodded. I didn't know if my plan would work. Hell, I didn't know if we were just out having a little ride that Mr. Masterson was going to end any second with the press of a button, then laugh at us while his goons dragged us back to the mansion. But we had to hold on to some kind of hope.

All my hope deflated, however, when I saw the red-and-blue lights flashing behind me.

"Shit," I muttered.

"Caleb, you were speeding. Maybe he just wants to give you a ticket?" Jacey suggested. She sounded desperate.

Hell, we were desperate.

I pulled over and rolled down my window when the cop approached.

"Do you know how fast you were g-Caleb Killeen?" the policeman asked, surprised.

"Yes, sir," I replied, my trepidation a hard rock in my stomach.

The officer looked past me. "Jocelyn Collins?"

"Yes, sir," Jacey said.

"Get out of the vehicle," the officer ordered sternly.

Oh fuck. This was it. We were completely fucked. We were going back to the mansion and never getting out again. If Masterson let us live after the baby was born.

"Sir..." I began to plead.

"Out!" the officer barked.

I sighed and stepped out of the Prius. Jacey did as well, coming around the front of the car to stand beside me.

"Get in the back," the officer said.

I saw his partner come out of the police car and helpfully open the back door of the cops' vehicle with its cage.

"Sir..." I protested.

"In!" the officer snapped.

Jacey began to cry silently. I put my arm around her. There was no way we could outrun these cops. We'd get tazed for sure.

I helped Jacey into the back of the police car then got in next to her. The door shut ominously beside me.

Just out of curiosity, I tried the handle, but it was a futile effort. We were trapped.

Jacey leaned her head on my shoulder and kept up a steady stream of silent tears as we pulled away from the Prius. She'd come to the same conclusion.

We were fucked.

The first officer's partner picked up the CB handheld and called over the line. "We've got Caleb Killeen and Jocelyn Collins."

To my absolute shock, Darren replied, "Bring them to the field office. STAT."

I gaped. It was him. Even with the static, I knew it was Darren.

"Yes, sir," the second officer said.

Then we were peeling down the road, lights and sirens.

When we got to the field office in Minneapolis, the police officers rushed us out of the back of their vehicle and into the building.

Darren was right there to greet us. "I gotta say, I was afraid we weren't going to be able to extract you."

"You didn't. Will let us go," I said flatly.

Jacey's hand shot out with the thumb drive in her palm. "Here. Here's whatever you wanted. Will gave it to me. Now get us away from here."

Darren took the thumb drive with a smile. "All right, kids. You've done good. We'll get you somewhere safe."

Jacey sagged against me with relief.

I still had words, however. Words that bubbled up from within like lava. "You do know Jacey's pregnant with the spawn of Satan junior, right?"

Darren's smile faded. "Shit. Did he rape you?"

Jacey shook her head. "Invitro fertilization," she replied.

"Well, we can take care of that right here in Minnesota if you want to," Darren said. "I'll just make a call."

"No," Jacey responded.

Darren and I both stared at her. "No?"

"I basically promised Will I'd keep it. So no," Jacey said.

"Jacey, a child is a lifelong commitment," Darren warned. "Think carefully."

"I did," Jacey insisted. "I'm keeping it."

I pulled Jacey into a hug. "Okay, baby. We'll have his baby. If that's what you really want."

"That's what I really want," Jacey said.

Darren shrugged. "All right. Let's go get you to my office. You can wait there until WITSEC shows up."

We followed Darren through security and up the elevator to his office.

Darren plugged the thumb drive into his computer right away. "Just gotta do a virus scan, then I can see what Will gave you."

I didn't give a flying fuck about it anymore. I sat on a sofa with Jacey with one arm around her, the other resting over hers on her belly. "We're having a baby," I murmured in awe, kissing her hair.

"Probably a boy," Jacey responded. "He wanted an heir for his legacy, after all."

After two hours, the antivirus software was still crawling through whatever Will had given us, and I was beginning to wonder if Witness Protection was ever going to show up.

There was a loud beep, then Darren leaned closer to his screen, clicking around with his mouse.

"Shit. This is some good shit," Darren said, surprised.

"I kind of figured it would be," I replied. "Will's a stand up guy. Most of the time."

"I'm quadruple copying this. You never know who that bastard has in his pocket." Darren opened his desk and took out more thumb drives.

"Glad we could help,' I said sarcastically. "Now when do we get to leave?"

Darren looked up, then passed us to the door. "Now, I think."

Two plain-clothes agents with their badges on their hips walked into Darren's office.

"Caleb Killeen and Jocelyn Collins?" the female agent asked.

"Yes, ma'am," I answered for us.

"You are now under the protection of the United States Witness Protection Program. You'll be moved to another state and be given new identities. You will not set foot in Minnesota again, nor contact anyone you know until you've borne witness at trial. Do you understand?"

"Yes, ma'am. Sounds great," I said, relieved.

"Yes, ma'am," Jacey echoed.

The female agent nodded to Darren.

"These are good officers," Darren said. "Smith and Jamison. They're going to take good care of you."

"Perfect." I stood and put my arm around Jacey again. "Let's get out of here."

I SWAM up behind Jacey in our small pool and slid my hands under her bikini top, cupping her swollen breasts.

Jacey groaned. Her baby bump was seven months along and looked so cute. I kissed the back of her neck and pushed her bikini bottoms aside so I could slip my rigid cock inside her.

"Caleb..." Jacey moaned, bracing herself against the side of the pool.

I had to admit, Jacey being pregnant had its advantages. Like her bigger breasts. And her voracious appetite for sex.

I wondered if I should just keep her pregnant, get up in there right after she had our first, and make our second.

Well, technically it was Will's first, but I wasn't splitting hairs. For all that kid was ever going to know, I was his father. And proud to be so.

I started thrusting, and Jacey made noises like a wild animal, digging her fingernails into the concrete edge of the pool.

"You like that, baby? You like it when Daddy gives you cock?" I murmured hotly in her ear.

"Yesss..." Jacey hissed. "Give me more cock, Daddy."

I thrust harder, deeper, faster, groaning. Fuck, it was hot when she called me 'daddy.' She'd started when I got my head around the fact I was going to be a dad.

Jacey came with a yell. "Daddy, give me your hot cum!"

This woman was going to be the death of me. I shivered and ejaculated into my Jacey. She wrung me out, milking me for everything I may have stored in my balls.

"So, Mrs. Allan, did you like that?" I wheezed, clasping her hands on the edge of the pool to hold myself behind and inside her.

"Mhm," Jacey sighed. "I did, Mr. Allan." She turned her head and kissed me. "You make me so happy, Mark."

I smiled. "Right back at ya, Angela." I twitched her bikini top back into place as I heard Roy approaching the fence.

"Hey, you two!" he called, going on his toes to peek over. "We're having a barbecue for dinner. Want to come?"

"Sure," I shouted back when Jacey nodded. "Want us to bring anything?"

"Some of that potato salad Ange made last time would be great, if you've got the ingredients," Roy said.

Jacey giggled. "I still have ingredients."

"Great!" Roy responded and disappeared behind the fence once more.

Roy and Petra were our neighbors to the left. They were a nice couple in their fifties who had basically adopted us.

"You know you were still cock deep in me during that whole conversation, right?" Jacey admonished me.

"Not sorry," I replied, sticking out my tongue.

Jacey laughed.

I stayed there a while longer, just enjoying the closeness, then sighed and pulled out. "Better get inside so I can help you with that potato salad, Angela."

"True." Jacey stretched, making her tits with their peaked nipples stand out.

My mouth actually watered. "On second thought..." I said, grabbing for a breast.

Jacey swatted my hand. "Potato salad, Mr. Mark Allan."

I pouted but helped Jacey up the steps and out of the pool just the same. We toweled each other off, then went inside.

A few hours later, we walked next door to the Nelsons, Jacey wearing a beautiful lime green sundress perfect for the warm Arizona weather. It was actually a dry heat.

I came in shorts and a Hawaiian shirt, carrying a glass dish of the potato salad.

"Ange! Mark! So glad you could come," Petra said, running up to Jacey and giving her a hug. She took the potato salad off me and brought it to the table they had set up on their lanai.

Roy was already grilling steaks and chicken breasts. I went over to do the guy thing and watch him. I was sure he was doing a perfectly fine job, but I'd learned standing over a man at the grill and giving advice was kind of a thing.

"Beer?" Roy asked, tossing me one before I even answered.

"Thanks," I said and cracked the can open. I was just taking my first sip when two people I didn't recognize came walking through Roy's back gate.

"Oh, you came!" Petra beamed. After settling Jacey in a wicker chair at the table, she turned to the newcomers and gave both of them a hug. "Mark, Ange, these are our new neighbors, the Stanhopes. Leon and Gail."

"I'd been wondering who bought the place across from us." I walked over and shook Leon's hand, then Gail's. "Pleased to meet you both."

The new couple were probably in their forties, both with brown hair and brown eyes. They were rather nondescript except that Gail had a mole on her left cheek, sort of like Marilyn Monroe.

"Pleased to meet you as well," Leon replied.

Gail looked over at Jacey as Petra fawned over her, getting her a lemonade and making sure she wasn't getting too much sun. "How far along is she? About six months?"

"Seven," I said. "We're expecting the birth of a bouncing baby boy in April."

"How sweet." Gail went to go see Jacey.

Leon followed me back over to the grill, and, per custom, we gave Roy advice while he turned the steaks and the chicken.

Once all was ready, Roy brought the meat to the table, and we all sat down and started serving each other up.

I cut Jacey's steak for her, kissing her on the cheek.

"Well, aren't you two cuter than a puddle of puppies," Leon said.

Jacey turned pale and dropped her lemonade.

The glass shattered on the ground.

End of Book 2

Want to keep reading? Chapter 1 of *Sequestered With My Stepbrother: Submitting to My Stepbrother Book 3* starts now!

SEQUESTERED WITH MY STEPBROTHER CHAPTER 1: TRAPPED IN SUBURBIA

-Jacey-

"Oh my dear! Are you all right?!" Petra asked, scurrying over to me. "Roy, get something to clean this up!"

I stared at Leon, who grinned at me. I didn't like the look of his grin.

Caleb put his arm around me, a fake smile plastered on his face. I knew it was a fake smile because I knew all his smiles. I also knew he'd heard what Leon said and come to the same conclusion.

I decided I needed to up my game, too. My smile shook, but I managed to put one on my face. "I'm sorry, Petra. It slipped right out of my hand."

"Condensation," Caleb added.

"Of course, my dear," Petra said sympathetically. "Roy!"

Roy hurried over with a broom and dustpan. Once the glass was cleaned up, he came over with the hose to just wash whatever was left into the lawn. "Petra, get Ange another glass. Can't have her dehydrating in her condition."

"No, we can't." Gail quite rudely rubbed my belly.

"Please don't do that without asking." Caleb defended me.

I clutched the edge of his shirt, using my hold on him to ground myself.

Petra came over with another glass and patted Jacey on the back. "Drink up, dear. And don't worry about the glass. I've always hated that set."

"Hey! My mother gave those to us!" Roy protested.

"All the more reason to hate it," Petra muttered and gave us a wink.

Caleb went back to cutting my steak, but I knew he was eyeing Leon and Gail. Were we in danger? Should we call Darren?

We'd been very fortunate in the fact that Darren had taken over overseeing our witness protection arrangements himself, not trusting anyone else to do it.

"Mark, do you think you should make that call?" I whispered. "The one to Dad? He's not feeling very well."

Caleb nodded and stood, pulling a cell phone out of his pocket. "I'm sorry, will you excuse me a moment?"

"I think you should call your dad later," Leon smiled, but there was a significant look in his eyes. "Pretty sure he's not home right now on a lovely day like this."

"Pretty sure he won't be home for a while," Gail murmured when Roy and Petra began bickering over the fruit salad.

Oh God. Had something happened to Darren?!

Caleb's eyes slid to Roy and Petra. Satisfied they weren't listening, he speared Leon with a glare. "What do you want?"

"Just to see the little bundle of joy is being well taken care of." Gail trilled a laugh. But her eyes were hard, dead.

I wondered if these were hired mercenaries. Whatever they were, they felt dangerous.

Caleb must have felt the same way because his arm around me tightened. "The bundle of joy isn't due for another two months. But he's doing just fine, thank you."

"Oh, we know. We've been keeping track," Leon said.

I let out a low whimper, and Caleb went white with rage. "If you don't leave us alone, it could hurt the baby," he hissed.

"Mr. Masterson thought it was about time you came home. I hope you enjoyed your vacation," Gail smirked.

"Where's Darren?" I blurted.

"Who's Darren?" Petra asked.

None of us had even realized the Hendersons had finished fighting.

"A mutual friend we just realized we have. Back in Minnesota," Leon said easily.

"He's been sick lately," Gail lamented. "Laid up in the hospital, poor thing. He had a terrible accident. He might have even suffered a brain injury." She looked at Caleb. "It's so horrible when bad things happen to good friends."

Leon was eyeing the Hendersons speculatively.

I dug my nails into Caleb's thigh.

"It is horrible. Luckily, it doesn't happen that often. In fact, I don't think it'll happen again for a long time," Caleb said.

"No. Not for a long time. But you really should go visit Darren. We can make all the arrangements. We wouldn't want to put any more stress on poor Angela here than we already have," Gail replied, examining her nails.

"Oh, you need to go to Minnesota to visit your friend?" Petra asked.

Roy was frowning now. I think he was getting the idea that something was amiss.

Please don't say anything. Please don't say anything, I silently begged, hoping either Roy or God could hear me.

"Hey, is something going on here? You're looking pretty squirrely, Mark. Are you guys upsetting Angela? She's pregnant, you know. If you're going to be doing upsetting things and having upsetting conversations, you can lea—" Roy began.

Leon pulled out a gun with a silencer on it and shot Roy in the forehead.

"No!" I screamed.

Caleb shot up to stop Leon, but Gail grabbed him by the shirt, and Leon quickly dispatched Petra as well.

"I wouldn't mess with Leon, Caleb," Gail said flatly.

To illustrate her point, Leon pointed his gun at Caleb.

I threw myself in front of him. "No, no!"

"We should get going," Gail added in a bored tone while Leon winked at us and put his gun back in an arm holster under his Hawaiian shirt. "I'm sure Jacey is quite upset now, and since we don't want her going into labor while we're in Arizona, time is of the essence."

"She shouldn't fly," Caleb said, sitting back down and embracing me. "Especially now that you've upset her."

"Too bad. We've already got the doctor's note. She's only seven months along. That's six weeks before they'd stop her from flying," Leon snorted. He grabbed me roughly by the arm.

I squeaked in pain.

Gail rolled her eyes. "I swear, Leon, you have the delicacy of an elephant." She swatted Leon's hand off me. "You, get her ready to go," she barked at Caleb.

Caleb glared at her but stood and helped me to my feet. He held me against him, rubbing his hands up and down my back. "It's going to be okay," he whispered in my ear. "Everything's going to be okay."

I hiccuped a sob but let Caleb comfort me. I knew as long as I had him, everything would be fine.

Gail and Leon quickly spirited us away in a black sedan from the Hendersons' house. I felt sick to my stomach over what had happened to them, and between the horror of it and pregnancy hormones, I couldn't stop crying.

At the airport, I got several strange looks. Caleb just held me and pasted on his fake smile. "Hormones," he said to those who asked. "What are you gonna do?"

Gail and Leon got us through the airport rather quickly and out to a private jet. I stumbled when I saw Mr. Masterson coming down the stairs to greet us, Will in his wake.

"Thought you could escape forever, did you?" Mr. Masterson asked pleasantly. Will just looked down at the tarmac. "Well, you were wrong about that, weren't you?"

"Yes, sir," I said quietly.

"What do you want, Masterson?" Caleb seethed.

Mr. Masterson raised an eyebrow. "Caleb, you're not that dense. You know what I want."

I put my hands protectively over my belly, and Caleb put a hand over mine.

"You're not getting my son," Caleb hissed.

"Oh, but it's Will's son. I made sure of that," Mr. Masterson chuckled. "And yes, I am getting him. His name will be William Masterson as well. Traditions are important, you see."

"So, in vitro fertilization on someone who doesn't want to be pregnant, an eighteen-year-old girl, no less, is somehow a tradition?" Caleb said, glowering at Mr. Masterson. "And how do you know she didn't miscarry, and we're having my son?"

"Caleb, Caleb, Caleb. You try so hard," Mr. Masterson tsked. "But you're just out of your league. She's a piss poor liar, and you're not much better."

Caleb held me close. "Leave us alone, Masterson."

"And you and I both know that won't be happening. Come on, now. Up on the plane you go." Mr. Masterson motioned for us to follow him onto the plane.

Will could barely look at us. He limped onto the plane as well.

"Oh God, what did Mr. Masterson do to him?" I gasped to Caleb as we followed our captor and my baby's father onto the plane.

"Nothing he won't get used to," Mr. Masterson said.

Gail and Leon followed us onto the plane and sat near us.

Will started to sit down by his father, but Mr. Masterson gave him a sharp look. "Tell your friends of your adventures, Will. Go on. Go sit by them."

With a wince, Will hobbled over to us. He sat down across from Caleb, his eyes on the floor.

"Will?" Caleb asked.

"Father had my legs broken." Will said softly. His eyes were swimming with tears when he looked up at us. "I won't be able to help you again."

I reached across the space between us and took his hand. "It's all right. You tried. I can't imagine what you've been through."

Will shivered. "It was worth it," he replied in a low tone. "Or at least it would have been if Father hadn't found you. Darren... Darren is in the ICU. He held out for so long."

A tear rolled down my cheek, and Caleb rubbed the back of my neck. "Is he going to be okay?"

"I don't think so," Will whispered.

I closed my eyes against the tears, but they still rolled hot down my cheeks.

"Jacey," Will said, looking stricken. "There's more."

"How much more can there be?" Caleb grunted, but I patted his thigh to tell him to let Will continue.

"Father's taken your father..." Will turned to Caleb. "... and your mother hostage. And... and the little one, too. Timothy."

"Our little brother?" I gasped.

"Is he healthy?" Caleb asked.

"Timothy's fine. Your parents are fine. They're just living at the mansion, like you will be," Will mumbled.

Caleb laughed mirthlessly. "One big happy family, then."

Will looked at me, then back at the ground. "We'll be having another after this one."

"I-I sort of guessed," I whispered.

"Great," Caleb said angrily. "That's just great."

"Father doesn't want to pay for in vitro again," Will went on.

I felt the blood drain from my face. "What?"

"Oh, that's not happening," Caleb insisted. "That's not happening at all."

"Do you want to live?" Will asked.

Caleb scowled, but finally nodded his head.

"Father said it wasn't necessary to keep you alive, but I've convinced him otherwise. I said you'd be good about it," Will said. "Please, please don't make a liar out of me. I don't want him to have you killed. And I sure as hell don't want you to end up like Darren."

"When do I have to start being 'good about it'?" Caleb inquired bitterly.

"After Jacey has our son," Will responded. "Father doesn't want anything to interfere with that."

"I'm sure he doesn't." Caleb put his arm possessively around me.

Will hung his head. "I'm sorry I failed."

"Hey." Caleb bumped Will's ankle with his boat shoe. "You did all you could. And so did Darren. Your dad's just a bigger prick than anyone realized."

Will smiled just a little at that. "I promise I'll be good to her," he vowed to Caleb. Then he blushed and turned to me. "I promise I'll be good to you."

"I know. You're a good guy, Will," I replied softly.

"I'm glad you think so. I don't feel like a good guy. In two months, I'm going to be putting my dick in my best friend's girl," Will said gloomily. "I don't know what my father's obsession is with you. I really don't."

"She's pretty, she's available, and no one will miss her if something happens to her," Mr. Masterson piped up.

"I'll miss her," Caleb growled.

"You are inconsequential. I think you'd better take a leaf out of Will's book. Keep your head down and shut up," Mr. Masterson advised.

Caleb's hands balled into fists, but I gripped his thigh before he could say anything. "Let's just try to get through this," I breathed in his ear. "Please, don't get yourself killed."

"Yeah," Will said. "Please don't get yourself killed."

Keep reading! Find Sequestered With My Stepbrother: Submitting to My Stepbrother Book 3 here!

ALSO BY M. FRANCIS HASTINGS

Once Bitten

Submitting to My Stepbrother series

Stranded With My Stepbrother

Snatched With My Stepbrother

Sequestered With My Stepbrother

Subpoenaed With My Stepbrother

The Beguiling Baronets series

Deceiving the Duke

Dream Mates

Dream Weaver

Dream Reader

Sign up for my newsletter here: https://subscribepage.io/TfsA3A